Picture Not So Perfect

Stephanie Jane O'Neil

WRITTEN
WITH LOVE
by Stephanie O'Neil

COPYRIGHT

Picture Not So Perfect, by Stephanie Jane O'Neil

First paperback edition November 2021

Book design by Danielle Greaves

Editing by Laura Simms & Beth Hale

ISBN 978-1-9168973-4-2 (paperback)

ISBN 978-1-9168973-3-5 (ebook)

www.stephaniejaneoneil.com

DEDICATION

To Tracey O'Neil, who died December 16th after a long battle. I love you. This book is dedicated to you.

To Richard Daniel, who fought hard till the end. We love you. This book is dedicated to you.

To those who fight hard, and can't make another Christmas; this is for you.

ACKNOWLEDGMENTS

I would like to thank everyone who has supported me so far on my journey to becoming a published author.

This book would not have been possible without my friend Laura, who worked tirelessly to help me edit the manuscript.

It would also not have been possible without support from my boyfriend, Jay, who stayed up late many nights helping me format, and provide encouragement when I felt like giving up.

Thank you to my cover designer, Danielle Greaves, for bringing my ideas to life, and to Beth Hale and my beta readers for helping turn a manuscript into the novel you're reading today.

I'd also like to thank my friends and family for their endless love and support. You know who you are.

Now…

Prepare to fall in love this Christmas...

CONTENTS

Picture Not So Perfect

CHAPTER ONE

Christmas sucks.

Some might think Christmas in the city is heaven, but not me.

In fact, I truly believe the entirety of December had been designed to annoy me.

As I walk through my hometown of Cardiff, everything that usually brings me comfort now irritates me. The commotion of life usually allowed me to forget about the stress in my life. But not during this time of the year. Everything about this awful holiday is a terrible reminder of what I have lost.

I keep my head down as I trudge through the slush, trying desperately to ignore the surrounding festivities. I stick my earphones in as far as they can go and I play my music loudly to drown out the carol singers and the sound of festive shoppers, wasting all of their hard-earned money on gifts that most people discard without a thought, to be buried in the far corner of the spare room.

The snow is coming down a lot heavier than I like, and I attempt to shield my camera equipment under my thick coat. No matter how many cosy items of clothing I put on, it still felt like I was perpetually cold. The chill of winter is truly upon me, and I hate it. As I make my way past the enormous Christmas trees and the strings of lights wrapped around every lamp post and fence, I wish I was somewhere warm. Perhaps a hot beach in Australia, where I could sunbathe and relax against graceful palm trees instead of being assaulted by the garish red, green, and gold covering every Christmas tree.

I finally reach my apartment, and I can't feel happier. Since December first hit, I have had a surge in Christmas photoshoot requests, and even though I need the money terribly, all I want to do is stay in my apartment and hibernate until January. Unfortunately, we can't all get what we want.

I brush the snow off my shoes before I walk through my apartment doors, and I am filled with relief at the sight of my gloriously undecorated living room, containing no Christmas tree, no messy tinsel, and no annoying flashing lights. This is normal for me. I know that once I come home, I can shut out all of the festive crap and pretend that this season doesn't exist.

Placing my boots on the shoe rack beside my front door, I pick up the mail on the floor and sift through it. I'm not sure why I bother checking my mail in December because it is only ever obnoxiously cheery Christmas cards.

Heading to the bin, I chuck the cards away without opening them and, as I do, I see my voicemail machine is flashing with a new message. I press 'Play' and continue scanning through the rest of my mail.

"Holly, it's your dad here." He pauses, his voice is quiet and unsure. I put the rest of the post down on the table as I listen. I know what this message is going to be about, and each year it feels harder to decline.

"I'm just calling to invite you for Christmas dinner again. It would mean a lot to me if you could stay for a few nights." His voice trails off as he considers the next thing he wants to say.

"Um, I know you're busy, but it would be lovely to see you. We missed you last year and the years before that, and... I think it's time we get past this." This time, his voice shakes with desperation. Each year, the hope from his voice slowly vanishes, replaced with sighs and hesitations, and each year, I still hate it.

"Call me back," He pauses again. "Please." The line goes dead and the message ends.

I stand there for a minute as I process the call. Every year, the same feelings shoot through me; a tightness in my chest and a headache which seems to last for hours. I still haven't identified whether it was guilt, frustration, or both. I want to spend the holidays with my family, but I just can't face it. It is all coming back to me, and I would do anything to forget about it.

Hearing my father's voice reminds me of my mother and that fateful December 17th. That date will forever be etched in my brain as the day my mother died nine years ago. I was fourteen at the time and I have not been able to escape the sense of loss I have felt since.

One of my fondest memories of her is her passion and love for Christmas. I can remember when I was a kid how she would dance around the living room with me in her arms, my father joining in when he walked into the room. She would eat cookies as she decorated the tree, and she would hand me the lights and decorations to complete the bottom branches of the tree because I couldn't reach any higher. My mother, Tracey, adored Christmas. That's why she named me Holly. She loved everything to do with December and used to say that holly was the most festive plant to be found.

The day she died was the day the joy and cheer in my life disappeared. The world suddenly seemed dull and disappointing.

Not wanting to upset myself on the subject that has tormented me for years, I try to find something else to occupy myself with. Usually, that is watching trash TV.

I flick through dozens of channels, and they are all plagued with Christmas series and films. I can't catch a break this time of year. There is no chance I can forget how lonely the holidays make me. Even my usual mind-numbing programmes aren't offering me their usual solace.

I get up from the sofa and head over to my wine rack, which contains quite a delicious selection. Pouring myself a glass, I can't help but look over at my answering machine. It is still flashing because I hadn't deleted the message. It is the same each year. Like heart-wrenching clockwork.

I always dread phoning my father back because each time my excuses are less and less believable, and each time I can hear him lose a little more hope. There's part of me that wants to be a part of his family, but something deep down holds me back. Every time I see a picture of him with his new family, my jaw clenches and the bitterness grows bigger inside of me.

Well, "new" is a controversial term. He met his wife three years after my mother passed, and they have two children. His wife is currently pregnant with their third child, and I always wonder how he could move on so quickly. Three years may not sound that short a time, but I'm still not over her death. So how can he be? How can he love again after loving someone so perfect for him? How can he start a new family when I am still here? I can't wrap my head around it.

It's been nine years since our lives changed and I lost my biggest cheerleader, best friend, and role model. Some days I struggle to remember her face. Other days I see her so clearly, it's as if she were here with me now. It's emotionally exhausting to have this conflict within me all of the time.

Still staring at the phone, I can't think of an excuse which doesn't make me look even more awful than the year before. I am running from my guilt and grief and it is all catching up to me.

I decide to put off the conversation for another hour because I can't face it right now. I place a throw over the answering machine to hide the obnoxious flashing and grab my leftovers from the fridge.

I take one bite of my pasta and the phone rings.

Seriously, can a girl not get a little peace to eat her pasta? I have been looking forward to this all day.

I let it go to voicemail.

"Hey, Holly. It's me again." It is my father. I can hear his kids in the background and his wife Sara telling them to stop pulling on the tree.

"I was hoping I could catch you as you got in from work. Did you hear my message?" He pauses, hoping I'll answer. I don't. He sighs. "I want to know what your decision is?" He pauses again.

"I know this is a difficult time for you, but you need to start enjoying your life again. I'm not sure what has made you feel as if you're not part of this family because you are." He pauses again, and I hold my breath.

"We want you here. All of us, not just me."

I can feel tears threatening to fall from my eyes, and my throat closes up. I place my pasta down on the side and take a few deep breaths, trying to calm myself.

His breathing is ragged and I can tell he is trying to calm himself.

"We would really love to see you here. If you're there, please pick up." I pace as I try to decide what I am going to do. My stomach sinks the longer he waits and the longer I pace.

"I guess you're not there." His voice hitches, and upon hearing that, I want to dash to the phone, and to pick up but I don't. He sighs heavily and the phone cuts out.

Standing there for a minute, my limbs heavy and my heart aching as I blink away the tears. I am having a hard time not calling him back, but I can't make myself do it. I'm not ready to pretend to be a family without my mother.

Shaking myself off, I pick up my pasta and continue eating. I turn the TV back on and switch over to Netflix.

I sit down and press play on a series I've seen before, trying to forget about this stupid holiday, my non-existent family, and the fact I am motherless. Thankfully, it works, mostly.

I am halfway through the show and have almost finished my pasta when a text comes through on my phone. It's from Callum. Oh God, another thing I don't want to think about right now.

I've had a few dates with him, and I find him slightly dull and too needy. I'm not sure why I have such bad luck with guys.

I have never been in a long term, serious relationship because I meet guys who are needy, boring, or creepy. Or they have gigantic noses or colossal heads.

I am better off alone.

His text reads, '*Holly! Would you fancy meeting up tomorrow for a coffee?*'

I roll my eyes and delete the message and his number. It's for the best. He can find someone who appreciates his neediness, so I am really doing him a huge favour.

I press play on my show and sit there in my apartment alone, just how I like it.

I increase the volume because I can hear people out in the street laughing and being raucous. It is typical this time of year.

Hours go by, and I am still unsure whether I will accept or decline my father's request. I want to accept, but something is telling me that it is a terrible idea. I'm not sure if I can deal with playing happy family with people I barely know. It hurts that I am the only one who can see that it had broken our family when my mother passed away.

I walk around the apartment, distracting myself with some cleaning, trying to silence my mind. I eventually start dusting the window, and I can't help but look through its frosty glass. It is still snowing in Wales, and the snow is settling upon the rooftops, tops of cars, and a little dust on the roads. Christmas lights are glistening and from my apartment, I can see Winter Wonderland and the Christmas markets. There are carol singers belting out Christmas hymns, and I can see several people browsing around some stalls and buying treats. Some with their partner's arms around their waist in a loving embrace.

All I can think about is how bored they must be to entertain the idea of Christmas. Yes, Christmas decorations and colourful shop displays are beautiful to look at, but it is nothing more than a money scheme from big corporations.

I close the blinds to shut out the world, and I turn in for the night. I will phone my father back in the morning and deal with the headache and heartache that comes with declining his request then. Right now, I'm too exhausted.

I brush my teeth, put on my freshly laundered pyjamas and wash my face. I can't sleep without some music playing in the background, so I turn on the speaker beside my bed and load up my "Shut off the world" playlist. Carrying out my typical bedtime routine helps me to feel calmer.

I have just gotten under the covers and put my sleeping mask on when I hear a *ping* from my phone.

Christ, can't I get any peace? As I think that, I laugh. I'm alone all year and mostly get radio silence. In fact, people hand peace to me on tap, so why is it that during Christmas time, the one time of year I want peace, everyone wants to get ahold of me?

With what I can only describe as a very unattractive groan, I turn over and fumble around for my phone from my bedside table. When I don't find it, I groan again and rip off my sleeping mask.

I'm worried that it might be another guilt-inducing text or voicemail from my father, and that is the last thing I need right now.

It isn't a text message I received; it is a photoshoot request from my booking form. I sit up in bed and click on the message so I can see more information.

"New Request: 3 days, England, Cotswolds, Friday 17- Monday 20th December, £1,650, accommodation and travel included. Confirm the booking ASAP."

I sit up, practically kneeling in bed as I look at that request and price. It is by far the most I will have ever made on a single photo shoot. Travel and accommodation included. It is basically a free holiday with very little work.

It is also the furthest I will have travelled for any photoshoot. Ever. Usually I'm asked to go to Cardiff or Bristol, somewhere more local.

I click on the link to approve or decline the request, hoping it will have a note from the client and a generalisation of where it would be. I will only get the specific postcode when I approve the request.

Once the page loads, I go into 'Photoshoot Notes'

'Hi! My mother wants photos over the festive period. Are you available? I know it's short notice, but we saw your portfolio and loved your work.'

Reading the brief note, I find myself considering it. I am available and I can go. There is nothing stopping me. It will give me a real excuse to decline my father's invitation, guilt free, and it will get me out of my apartment for Christmas. It'll allow me to avoid another lonely, disappointing Christmas because I will be around people who expect no emotional investment from me. I will be there to work and that seems better than going to my father's and feeling obligated to be something I'm not. I would be getting paid to escape the tortuous Christmas cycle. My prayers have been answered.

But, the longer I stare at the phone and the message, I start questioning my decision. It is far away, and it has been snowing extremely hard lately. What if I dislike the family? I guess I can just book a train home. Each time I create a reason not to go, my mind supplies solutions and ways around things.

It is Thursday 16th December. I glance at my clock, and it tells me it is almost ten at night. That means I have a few hours to decide. I am hyper-aware I have to book my train and because it is Christmas, there won't be much availability.

Jumping up out of bed, I go to my computer, sit down, and log in. Going into my booking request, I have the option to email the client.

I open up a blank email, and the cursor flashes.

From: Ohsnapphotography@gmail.com
To: Justinwilliams@gmail.com
Hello Justin,

I'm the photographer you've requested for 17th December. I'm emailing to receive more information. Please can you answer the following questions:

What kind of photographs are you looking for? Could you tell me more about the shoots?

Are the photographs for yourself? Or for someone else?

Thank you.

Oh Snap! Photography.

I hope I will get a response tonight, as the request has just come through, and I would have to be there tomorrow. It is a very time sensitive request. As I wait for the reply, I feel restless and need something to do, so I open up a second tab and begin searching up the Cotswolds in England.

It is just a couple of hours on the train from Cardiff. That isn't too bad and I can update my photography website while I am on the train. I have a ton of administration work I need to do.

I continue to search up the Cotswolds on Google and browse through images to see what it looks like. The first images that show up are of quaint little towns lined with cottages made from stone.

I scroll down further and come across an image which has a cottage covered in snow, and it looks like a typical Christmas town. It doesn't look real to me; almost synthetic. Seeing this image almost makes me want to pull out. I can't deal with the festive feel in Wales, let alone in the town that Christmas threw up on.

Before I can scroll anymore, a new email notification comes through, startling me out of my Christmas-induced foul mood.

It surprises me to see how quickly they got back to me, but I feel relieved that I can get some answers.

From: Justinwilliam@gmail.com
To: Ohsnapphotography@gmail.com
Hi there,
Of course. My family has a lot of Christmas traditions and my sister was recently engaged. My fam-

ily (mother) would like festive photos, with a few photos of the happy couple. Unfortunately my grandmother is ill, so it would mainly be at the house.

I'll be making the arrangements for my mother. She's not the best with technology.

Justin.

I hope it isn't serious, because I know what it is like to lose someone close to you. I don't want to pry, or throw unwanted heaps of sympathy his way, because I hated it when that happened to me. So I keep it short and sweet and move on.

From: Ohsnapphotography@gmail.com
To: Justinwilliams@gmail.com
Hi Justin,

My father isn't the best with technology either. He's just about able to type an email, so I completely understand. And I'm sorry to hear that. I can certainly do this for you. From your request, I can see you live in the Cotswolds in England, is that correct?

Oh Snap! Photography.

From: Justinwilliams@gmail.com
To: Ohsnapphotography@gmail.com
Hi there,

That's great!

Does this mean you've accepted the request?

And yes, we live in Gloucestershire.

Justin.

Does it?

This question holds a lot of weight. Usually I have no issues accepting a job, especially one that is paying so generously. If I think about it, when will this happen again?

Staring at the blinking cursor, I am unsure.

Did I really want to spend Christmas with another family?

As I am sitting here debating whether I should go, my mind starts replaying the memories I have of past Christmas photoshoots.

I remember two Christmases ago; I photographed Santa and his elves for a kid's birthday party at St. Davids in Cardiff. Half way through the shoot, I, and many of the parents, realised Santa was extremely drunk. I guess the first indicator was when he fell over the presents and took out a few elves on the way down.

I also remember the time I went to another family's house for a family Christmas shoot, and all they did was bicker. The father was clearly texting his mistress, and I caught the grandmother sneaking some pills in the kitchen.

It's safe to say not all of my shoots are straightforward and easy going.

Thousands of questions are going around in my head: What do I do? Should I stay? Should I go? What happens next?

After a few minutes of racking my brain and seriously considering the pros and cons I decided.

I am going.

From: Ohsnapphotography@gmail.com
To: Justinwilliams@gmail.com
Hi Justin,

Yes. I have just accepted the request, so you should receive a notification of acceptance shortly. I'll look into booking a train ticket.

Oh Snap! Photography.

As I send that email, my chest feels lighter, and a jolt of energy rushes through me. I jump onto the train website almost immediately and search for the earliest train I could get to, while considering the time I will have to pack. The earliest ticket I can get is one o'clock, getting me there at two thirty.

That will give me plenty of time to pack in the morning and sort everything out if I wake up early.

Another message comes through.

From: Justinwilliams@gmail.com
To: Ohsnapphotography@gmail.com
Hi there,
I'm confirming I have received the acceptance.

Justin.

From: Ohsnapphotography@gmail.com
To: Justinwilliams@gmail.com
Hi Justin,
I've had a look at train tickets, and it should take me an hour or so by train.

Oh Snap! Photography.

I sit closer to the desk, and as I am waiting for his response, I flick through photos of the Cotswolds and I start reading articles about what there is to do. Maybe I can explore when I'm not needed at the house for photographs, and it will mean they won't feel the need to rope me into any of the festive Christmas crap.

From: Justinwilliams@gmail.com
To: Ohsnapphotography@gmail.com
Hi there,
I live about thirty minutes from the station, so I would be more than happy to pick you up from that point.
Justin.

From: Ohsnapphotography@gmail.com
To: Justinwilliams@gmail.com
Hi Justin,
Okay, sounds like a plan. I'll book the ticket now.
Oh Snap! Photography.

And I do.
Checking the time, I noticed it was midnight. If I have any chance of being remotely awake tomorrow at seven in the morning, I am going to need to sleep right now.
Firing off one last email to confirm I have the ticket and what time I will arrive, I head back to the comfort of my bed and go to sleep. Or at least I try to, but the nerves and excitement are a major obstacle.

CHAPTER TWO

Morning arrives an to no one's surprise, I'm tired. I didn't sleep at all last night, as my body had been vibrating with ideas and thoughts about today.

I crawl out of bed after turning my alarm off and sit on my bed for a good five minutes before I stand, make my way to the window, and open the curtains. It does not surprise me to see snow is still falling and there is no hint of the sun showing its face any time soon. It is still dark outside, but the city of Cardiff is illuminated by colourful Christmas lights, street lights, and beaming headlights of cars as they drive past.

It is exceptionally chilly this morning, so I head over to my wardrobe and throw on the cosiest dressing gown to exist. This dressing gown is fluffy, warm, it has a hood and, best of all, deep and spacious pockets. This dressing gown has seen me through a few bad days and nights, and it is still as emotionally supportive as the day I bought it. This was definitely coming with me.

Walking into the living room, I see the flashing of the answering machine and I know that it is time I phone my father.

Grabbing the phone, I tap in his number and hold my breath as it begins ringing.

I know he will be up because he has always been an early bird. I definitely didn't get that from him. My mother was the night owl and would sleep in until at least midday. To my father, that was a nuisance. He always wanted to get started with the day as soon as the sun rose, but my mother wanted to work into the early hours of the morning, which meant she wouldn't sleep until three in the morning. But, they loved the same shows and they were both so in love. If they went to get themselves a drink, they would always return with two glasses. They would share everything with each other, and they never went to bed upset.

She was an extremely creative person, where-as my dad considered himself as a realist. They were so different, yet so similar, and that's why they worked so well together. They balanced each other out regardless of their pet peeves.

"Hello?" My father's voice sounds as if he is out of breath. Of course, he likes to work out early in the morning.

"Hi, Dad, it's Holly."

"Holly, hi! How are you? How have you been?" He sounds ecstatic to hear my voice, and I can't really understand why. It isn't like I'm completely MIA all the time. I just don't fancy playing happy families during the one holiday I hate.

"I've been good. Are you and the family okay?" I don't particularly care. I just know it is a form-ality to ask such things.

"Good, good! Yeah, we're all okay. The kids have been so excited about Christmas. We can't seem to get them to sleep and when we can, it snows, so they want to rush outside in their pyjamas and make snow angels," he laughs. This puts a knot in my stomach and I find it a little harder to swallow. It's as if I'm jealous, but I have no real reason to be.

"Sounds like fun." I try to put more enthusi-asm than I actually feel into my voice.

"Yeah, it is." He can tell it isn't sincere. "Did you get my message?" he asks, almost as if he is afraid of my answer. The knot tightens and my heart starts beating a little harder. Why am I always feeling this way? I have gone years and years with this guilt and jealousy or whatever the hell this is, and I am fed up.

"Yeah, I got your message, and that's why I'm calling you so early." I pause, needing another second to process and practice what I am going to say.

"I received a photoshoot request last night," I say, trailing off, prolonging the inevitable.

"That's great! When is it?" he asks, his voice full of pride. I try my absolute hardest to push the guilt down.

"Today," is all I can say.

"Where is it?"

"The shoot is in England, Dad."

"Oh." He goes quiet for a minute or two, and I wait until he responds.

"Yeah."

We both go quiet, and I hope he understands what I'm trying to say until he asks this next question.

"So you're coming over after the shoot?"

I move the phone away from me as my stomach drops and my eyes close, taking a deep breath, feeling awful about disappointing him.

"No, it's for three days. They're paying me a lot of money, and it's too good an opportunity to miss. My train is at one this afternoon," I say, trying to sound happy and excited, but having a feeling that I am failing miserably.

"Oh, I see."

I wait a minute to see if he will say anything else. He doesn't. Maybe if I explain the shoot in more detail, he'll understand why I've chosen to go.

"They seem lovely. They're paying for accommodation and travel, and they're paying me more than I would get in a month doing ten shoots."

"Yeah, I can see how that would help you out." His voice is flat and monotone, but I can tell he is trying to be supportive. It isn't like this is the first year I've declined. It will be like nothing has changed for him. He will go back to his family and they will have their Christmas traditions and forget I'm not there. They don't need me to have a lovely holiday.

In fact, I'm pretty sure I would just ruin it, anyway.

After a little longer trying to chat about something other than my avoidance of a family Christmas, we hang up, and I jump straight into packing. I need something to distract myself with.

I grab my suitcase out of my wardrobe and chuck it on my bed. I add extra jumpers and scarves because I know England is colder than Wales at the moment. Still, I'd rather be in sunny Australia. And that's on the other side of the world. Perfect.

Once I finish packing, it is almost nine in the morning. I have a while until I have to make the journey to the train station, so I make breakfast. Considering I am travelling today, I decide to treat myself.

I make pancakes.

I've noticed a pattern in my pancake making life. If I burn one or both of the sides, it always leads to a bad day, so this is a test to see how great or crap my day would go.

19

Burnt pancakes equals a bad day.

Golden, fluffy pancakes equals a good day.

Flipping the pancakes for the last time, I frown, not sure what's happened. I burned them on one side, but the other half is golden. I've never gotten that before, so I'm not sure what that was telling me about today. Does that make me slightly uncomfortable? Yes. But am I glad they aren't entirely burnt and I can actually enjoy them to some extent? Also yes.

After I finish my pancakes, I begin sorting the apartment out and ensuring I have everything I need for the journey. Especially my camera equipment. I learnt over the years to double, triple and quadruple check I had my camera equipment because I had been to many shoots where I had forgotten everything. Checking if my camera battery is full because yes, I had been to a shoot where I had forgotten to charge my battery. This definitely all makes me sound like an amateur, but let's be honest, mistakes ensure we learn.

I have everything, so I am ready to get going.

I head out the door and I can see my breath coming out as small, dense clouds with each breath I take. I remember when I was younger, I would use those clouds and pretend to smoke, much to my parents dismay.

I lock my door, turn around, and am again smacked in the face with the festivity outside. The snow has settled down for the moment, and I speed up, wanting to avoid the next onslaught of snow. It is cold enough without melting snow trickling down the back of my coat and freezing my neck. If I can help it, I will stay out of the snow as much as humanly possible.

As I turn the corner into Caroline Street, I see children making snow angels and chucking snowballs at their siblings.

I always wonder why people love the snow so much, especially in Cardiff, as it is a city with plenty of things to do. But I also know that Wales is notorious for its unpleasant weather. Eighty percent of the time we're plagued with rain, and nineteen percent we have mild/moderate sun. The last one percent is snow.

I can now see the train station and I can't help but overhear a couple talking as they jog towards the station.

"They say it's the worst storm we've had in years. We can't miss this train!" the girl says, carrying her suitcase as it won't roll in the slush currently covering the ground.

"I know, I think we'll just make it in time." Just as he says that, it starts snowing again. It isn't particularly heavy, but it is still an inconvenience. At least with the slush on the roads it will be unlikely for the snow to stick. People in Wales freak out at the first sign of snow on the roads, even though we definitely are not the country with the most snowfall. In fact, they rush off into the shops, buying bread and milk in bulk and schools shut one by one. After a day of heavy snow, it stops and we wonder what all the fuss was about. I am not cancelling my journey for a bit of snow.

I scan my ticket into the machine and enter the platform going to Gloucester. It is busy as people hurry around the station, talking about the snow and the weather warnings they had heard on the news. I completely ignore them and put on my headphones as I walk onto the platform.

As I enter the platform, there is a conductor who is swarmed with passengers.

I wonder why they are around him? Perhaps they are worried about the snow, scared to even get on the train. It is ridiculous.

Shaking my head, I check the screens showing the arrivals, and see the words '**CANCELLED**' in big, bold letters.

What? That can't be right. I've only just booked the bloody ticket.

Marching towards the conductor, I try to force my way through the crowd of panicked passengers and am bombarded with their complaints to the conductor.

"You have to get me on that train! I have to get back to my family!"

"My boss is going to kill me if I'm not at that meeting!"

"Surely there's something you could do. My mother is in the hospital and I don't want her to be alone for the holidays!"

Realising the conductor is not going to help in this situation, especially with having to handle the rest of the stressed out passengers, I haul my suitcase out of the crazed crowd and travel down the escalator and make my way to the reception.

"Excuse me?" I place my ticket on the table.

"I booked a ticket last night, and now it's cancelled. There must be some kind of mistake." The receptionist sighs, as if she is fed up with answering the same question. She chews gum and rolls her eyes, not even bothering to look at my ticket.

"I'm sorry, Miss. There's nothing I can do. They cancelled the trains because of the weather. I can refund your ticket," she said, smacking her lips and checking out her nails.

"No, I need to get on that train. It's for a job," I insist, growing more frustrated by the minute.

"Look, I'll tell you the same thing I've told everyone else. There's nothing I can do."

I cannot believe what I am hearing. I draw in a deep breath and try to approach this differently.

I check the woman's name tag.

"Look, Becky. I really need to get to Gloucester. Is there any way, any way at all, you could help me?" I muster up the sweetest voice I can in the hopes she can help me out.

Of course, it doesn't work. She doesn't once check her computer for a solution, or my ticket.

She sighs, rolling her eyes again. "Please step aside."

"You really shouldn't work in customer service, Becky," I spit, grabbing hold of my suitcase and forcing my way through the crowd who has now formed around the reception desk.

What the hell am I going to do?

CHAPTER THREE

As I sit on a bench inside the station, I pull out my phone and log into my emails. I'm not surprised the trains are cancelled. I didn't expect it would be easy to catch a last-minute train at Christmas, during snow, without a hitch. But I still hoped I would get lucky.

> **From**: Ohsnapphotography@gmail.com
> **To**: Justinwilliams@gmail.com
> Hi Justin,
> They have cancelled the trains. I'm sorry I can't take on this job, but the weather has made it impossible to reach you in time. I hope you find someone who can help you.
> Oh Snap! Photography.

As I send the email, I stand up feeling defeated and am about to head out of the station, when I see about thirty taxis lined up outside of the station. Why hadn't I thought of this earlier? A taxi! They never turn away from business.

I pick up my suitcase, not wanting it to slow me down by getting stuck in the grimy slush that filled the road, and bolt outside into the freezing cold snow. The first few taxis are taken as people haul their suitcases into the boot and jump inside the warmth of the car.

I trudge past at least seven taxis before I get to one with no passengers trying to get in. I knock on his window, praying he can get me to Gloucester. He rolls his window down.

"Can I help you?" The guy looks tired and fed up. I don't blame him. Christmas is *always* unnecessarily hectic.

"I need a taxi to get to Gloucester," I blurt, stating the obvious. Of course, I need a taxi or else why would I be knocking on this random man's window?

"I don't go that far." And he tries to roll up his window.

"No, wait!" I press my hand against the window, receiving a displeased look off the taxi driver. I remove my hand, muttering an apology, and turn on my charm.

"Please?" I beg, clasping my hands together. I can't back down now. I have never been this adventurous or spontaneous, and I am determined to get that job. It is great for my business.

"Sorry, but I finish in an hour, and it's been a hectic day. I want to get home and enjoy the holidays," he says and rolls his window back up.

"Where's your Christmas spirit?" I shout and bang on his roof, earning myself a few looks from passengers who are walking past me to get to the last taxis. Nope, I am getting a taxi.

I pick up my suitcase and try to push my way past a guy wearing a reindeer jumper who tries to barge me out of the way and a couple who are carrying bags full of Christmas gifts, to the point they are struggling to walk. They seem happy enough, whispering about their Christmas plans once they get home and who is going to wrap whose presents. It sounds like such a joyful life, yet I feel repulsed by it.

Trying to ignore their happiness and whispering, I finally edge round them, accidentally knocking into their bags.

"Hey!" they shout.

"I'm sorry!" I shout back.

I finally reach the taxi, and knock on the guy's window, hoping he can get me to Gloucester.

He smiles and opens his window.

"Where do you need to go?" he asks, cheerfully. Looking inside his car, I notice he has tinsel on his dashboard, and a Santa Claus bobble head. I ignore it, looking away.

"Hi! I was wondering if you could get me to Gloucester? I know it's a long drive, but-" He cuts me off.

"Gloucester? I live there!" he says, laughing. It is a literal Christmas miracle.

He unlocks his car without another word. I don't hesitate to put my suitcase in the boot and jump in the back, revelling in my good luck. This almost never happens to me.

Once I am settled in the back, I open up the window, wanting to know more about my miracle.

"If you live in Gloucester, why are you in Cardiff?" I ask, as he pulls out of the station.

"Because I had to drive someone from Gloucester to Cardiff," he replies, laughing as if I should've already known the answer. I roll my eyes and sit back in the seat, relishing in the warmth. I wipe away the condensation off the window with my sleeve, watching as the world speeds past. There is one good thing about a taxi: nobody will sit next to me, as I generally find it awkward. If I am on a train or a coach, I never refuse a seat to anyone, but I feel uncomfortable and wish that they would move the entire journey.

Luckily, I don't have that issue today.

As we drive, we pass a woman with a bright red coat carrying her baby in the snow. The baby is laughing and trying to catch the snow between their tiny hands. Before I know it, they disappeared.

I can't help but imagine what the family in England is like. Perhaps they're stuck up their own arse and won't notice if I disappear after every shoot, so I won't be forced into the Christmas traditions and festivities.

Justin seems nice. I wonder if he is as nice in person as he has been over email. Checking the time, I notice a new email from Justin.

From: Justinwilliams@gmail.com

To: Ohsnapphotography@gmail.com
Hi there,
Perhaps get a taxi or a coach? We're more than happy to pay for it. Let me know what's happening.
Justin.

I can't believe they would pay for a taxi. It will be a few hundred pounds, at least. I will never admit to Justin that this taxi will set me back, but I figure I can make the money back in this job. I'll work something out, I always do.

From: Ohsnapphotography@gmail.com
To: Justinwilliams@gmail.com
Hi Justin,
I'm in a taxi. I can't ask you to pay for it, it's too much.
I'll email you when I'm close to the station. See you soon.
Oh Snap! Photography.

The snow is sticking more the further out we go. I look out of the window onto the fields, which now hold thick layers of snow. It is picturesque, but it raises a few warning bells and the conversation I overheard from the couple running to the train station replays in my mind.
Shaking off my worries, I read another email from Justin.

From: Justinwilliams@gmail.com
To: Ohsnapphotography@gmail.com
Hi there,
Great! We want to pay for the taxi. Especially because it's so last minute, during Christmas!
Meet at the station as planned.
Justin.

They are very generous. I lean forward to the window and inform the driver where he can drop me. Grabbing my laptop, I distract myself with some photography admin work. I have to update my website with a couple new reviews I have received and add them to my online portfolio. I also have some editing to complete for a client, so this should last me until Gloucester.

Or so I hope.

***

"Almost there," the taxi man says. Rubbing my eyes, I log out of my laptop and pack it back into my carry on. I sent Justin an email about thirty minutes ago, confirming I was close. I have no new email from Justin saying he was leaving, so I hope he is there. I can feel myself becoming nervous as the station comes into view.

What if I dislike this family, and I'm stuck there for three days? Maybe they'll hate me and give me an awful, critical review? Considering they are paying me rather well, I can't afford to lose this potential client.

Another intrusive thought pops into my head, and I regret not requesting the taxi to drop me at the house. What if the car journey with Justin is awkward? At least if I get the taxi, I'm socially allowed to stay quiet and not obligated to partake in small talk and pleasantries, which made this journey so much better.

Perhaps I have made a mistake.

I peek out of the window, hoping to see if I can guess who Justin is. Maybe it is the guy with the checkered jacket? Or the guy who's wearing a knitted cardigan? Or even the guy with a Christmas jumper on?

No, it couldn't be any of these. Justin looks so different in my head, so maybe he isn't here yet?

The taxi is now parked outside the station. My heart is beating very quickly, and my mouth becomes incredibly dry.

"There we are, Miss. Cash or card?" he asks, turning around in his seat.

"I'm meeting a guy called Justin. He said he would pay, I just have to find him," I explained. The taxi man nods, pulling out a newspaper from the glove box and settling back into his seat.

I wipe the condensation off the window again and keep looking for any sign of Justin. At this moment, I wish I had emailed Justin to ask what he would be wearing, or at least where he would be waiting. It is too cold to stand around waiting for someone I don't know.

Before I can panic, a man walks towards the taxi. It's the guy wearing a Christmas jumper. Of course, he is the guy wearing a Christmas jumper, just my luck. I can't see any more of his features as the snow begins falling harder.

I get out of the taxi, greeted with freezing cold air. It hits my face so hard my eyes begin to water and goosebumps appear on my skin. It is incredibly frosty, the coldest day of winter, according to the news. The sky is white and specks of snowfall as the wind picks up. Each time a gust hits my face, it feels as if a thousand needles are piercing my skin. How can anyone live like this?

I am glad I brought extra coats, scarves, and gloves because I can tell I am in for a bitterly cold few days.

As we get closer, I scoff at the ridiculousness of his outfit. Walking towards him, I try to keep all judgement off my face. It is incredibly hard because the jumper has flashing lights embedded within it.

I give him a small wave as I approach. He immediately waves back, a friendly smile on his face.

"I'm assuming you're the photographer?" he asks, slightly shouting as the wind picks up.

"And I'm assuming you're Justin?" I shout back, snow getting into my mouth and eyes.

Justin laughs as I attempt to spit out the already melting snow. He leans towards the taxi's window and says something to the driver. I can't hear what they say, but my eyes widen when he pulls out a wad of notes and hands it to the driver with no qualms.

Before I can object to him paying that much money, Justin takes my suitcase out of the boot and the driver pulls away.

I pull my coat closer to me, struggling to see as the snow gets heavier.

"Yeah, I'm Justin, what's your name?" He drags my suitcase against the snow, which has stuck on the icy ground, and gently ushers me towards his car.

My photography page includes that my name was Holly in the 'about me' section in an extremely tiny font, right at the bottom, and I'm assuming he hadn't seen it.

"Grace," I lie. It is a split second decision, and I can't go back now. I hate my name and if I could help it, I would always say my name was Grace, which is my middle name. So technically I didn't lie.

Holly is such a cliche name, especially this time of year. Therefore, I make sure my business page has little to no mention of it.

"Nice to meet you, Grace. How was your journey?" he asks. His English accent is strong.

I have to roll my eyes when he isn't looking because I hate small talk. But I know it is important to some people, and I'd rather that than awkward silence.

"Minus the trains being cancelled and having to find a taxi in the freezing cold, it was good."

"Sorry about that. If I'd known the trains would be cancelled, I would've provided another form of transportation. We're supposed to have a storm soon, so that hasn't helped matters," he says, brushing the snow off his jumper.

The Christmas jumper is not giving off a good impression. It is cheesy, and I feel second-hand embarrassment from him wearing that jumper.

We are bombarded with more snow. It is coming down like a blizzard now, and I'm slightly worried about getting home.

I definitely can't afford the taxi back.

CHAPTER FOUR

We say nothing as we dash along the road, trying to avoid people doing the same. The snow is so heavy we can barely see the cars' headlights as they drive past.

Justin is leading me to his car, and I try my hardest to keep him in my sights. If I lose him, I'll be royally stuck.

Finally, a car's lights flash as Justin unlocks it, and I don't hesitate to open the door and jump straight in. I need to get away from that awful snow before I freeze to death.

He dashes straight to his boot and struggles as the wind and snow keeps the door shut.

I find it hilarious for the first two minutes and then I lose all feeling in my toes.

I check my phone and I'm dismayed to see that the temperature is one degree.

This is ridiculous! Not wanting to be stuck at the train station in a freezing cold car as the snow on the floor starts building, I get out of the car and practically throw my body against the wind to walk as snow barrels towards me. I have to keep my eyes partially closed and my head down to ease the assault.

Once I've reached Justin, I grab the handle and try to help him open the boot. It moves ever so slightly and I see that as an opportunity to pull with all my strength. I can feel the snow making its way down the back of my coat, and I have to physically stop myself from squealing.

The boot still hasn't budged. Justin leans in closer to me.

"Would you...get in the back.. and push the boot... inside?" he forces out. I'll do anything to leave here.

I nod and don't waste any time getting into the back. I am happy for a moment as I can't feel the wind and snow anymore.

I lean against the back seats and try to reach the boot door. My coat strains, extremely restricted, and my arms are frozen, so I can't reach it. Climbing over the back seats in a very disorganised and ungraceful manner, I reach for the boot and push from the inside. After a few seconds, the boot pops open, and snow and wind once again greet me as it rushes into the car.

Justin places my case into the boot and closes it as I climb back over the seats and scramble into the front. He gets in and closes the door.

We are both quiet for a second as we try to catch our breath, the car moving slightly as the wind bashes against the sides.

"Why didn't we just put your case on the back seat?" Justin asks, chuckling.

"I actually don't know." I laugh. My feet are soaking and I can't wait until I have a shower. Just thinking about a shower warms me up a little.

"Well, our way was a lot more fun," he grins, turning the keys.

"My freezing limbs would have to disagree with you there." He chuckles again and turns the heating on full. Now that we are both in the car, away from the battering wind and snow, I can see him. His eyes are blue, bright blue and his hair is brown, with light golden highlights running through it.

He says, "It'll take a minute to kick in, especially in this weather, but I have a blanket under the backseats if you want that?"

How sweet of him to ask. The gesture warms me, and I would be extremely stupid if I said no considering the fuss I've kicked up regarding the snow.

"I think I should or else I risk losing my fingers." He reaches around and fumbles for the blankets. As he does, I catch a whiff of his aftershave.

"Well, this is the least I could do after you helped me with the boot. I was thinking I would turn into a snowman."

"It is freezing, I wouldn't be surprised if you turned into Olaf!" I exclaim, rubbing my hands together and blowing into them, trying to regain some feeling.

He laughs, handing me a fluffy blanket, and places the car in first gear.

"Thank you." I wrap the blanket around me, up to my nose.

"I'm sure once you hit the main roads the snow should be easier to drive on." Looking at the roads right now, the snow is almost impossible to drive over. As there are no cars driving in or out of the station right now, there are no tyre tracks for us to follow or drive on, which makes it very difficult for Justin. I definitely don't envy him as I snuggle into the blanket.

"I hope so, it's still twenty minutes from my house. We just need to get to mine and ride this storm out," he says, briefly looking at me, a small smirk on his face. I wonder why he is smiling, but then realise it must be because he can only see the top of my head. I shroud the rest of me in the comfiest blanket I think I've ever wrapped around myself.

"At least you're with us for a few days. I'm sure this storm will calm down," he tries to reassure me. I say nothing, as I hope that is true. I am already worried about the snow, and my thoughts go to the couple in Cardiff station. What if they are right, and it is the worst storm the UK has seen in years? I could be stuck out here with a family I have never met, forced to spend even longer with these strangers.

Brushing that thought out of my mind, and the rest of the snow out of my hair, I try to distract myself.

"Do you mind?" I ask, reaching towards his radio.

"No, no, go ahead," he says, turning onto the main road. It is eerily quiet, but I was right; the snow isn't as bad on the main road. At least not yet.

I turn the radio on and immediately the news comes on.

"Today we saw the worst snowstorm in twenty-three years. We advise you to stay indoors unless essential."

Of course, the worst storm since the year I was born. It seems like Fate or Luck, or whatever you believe in, thinks my life is a huge comedy show. I change the station, but they are all playing Christmas music.

Groaning, I turn off the radio altogether, and I see Justin looking at me from the corner of my eye.

"Don't you like Christmas music?"

Oh great. Here it comes. The talk I was hoping to avoid this week. I am going to say I'm not the biggest fan of Christmas, and he is going to look at me as if I am crazy. This is how those conversations typically go.

What if I say nothing? What if I just say I'm not fancying music because I love hearing this obnoxious howling wind?

"I'm not the biggest fan of Christmas," I mutter, my big mouth has chosen for me. Now all I have to do is deal with his inevitable reaction.

"What?! You seriously hate Christmas?" He questions, aghast. There it is.

"I never said 'hate'. I just don't like Christmas. It's the same as people who hate Halloween or Valentine's day." I have rehearsed this argument so many times over the years, I can now say it without thinking.

"You said 'hate'," he challenges. I look at him as if he has grown several heads. What is he even talking about?

"No, I never said 'hate'. I just don't like Christmas."

"You said 'People who hate Halloween.'" he mimics and I scoff, wondering why that is relevant to the conversation. I don't hate Christmas, I just strongly dislike it.

"What do you *dislike* about Christmas, then?" he asks, as if he either thinks it is stupid I don't like Christmas or that I am joking. It is typical.

"I don't really want to talk about it." I knew I'd get this reaction, and I can't be bothered to explain myself anymore. I don't like Christmas and I doubt I'll change. In fact, I don't want to change.

"I'm sorry if I offended you. It's just rare to meet someone who doesn't like Christmas," he said as he glances over at me. I nod, not saying anything else, and we both fall into an uncomfortable silence.

The car vibrates and thumps as it swerves to the left slightly as if we have run over something.

"Crap." Justin slows down and pulls over.

"What? Did we run something over?" I ask, turning around, trying to see amidst the snow.

"I don't know, but my tyre pressure warning light has just come on. I'm going to have to go out and have a look." He doesn't hesitate to step out of the car, causing the interior light to come on. He closes the door, and the light goes out, leaving me in darkness.

He has only been gone a few seconds before my door opens, and cold air and snow barrells in, causing me to shiver.

"It's a flat tyre, I'm going to have to call someone!" he shouts, the wind howling around us.

Pulling his phone out and grunting some curses, he runs his fingers through his hair and shuts my door. He comes around the car, opens his door, and sits back into his seat, rubbing his hands to warm them back up.

"What's going on?" I ask, my breath clouding in front of me. It is starting to get really cold in this car, and I am not enjoying it.

'I have no service. Maybe I could walk home."

"No, that would take way too long. Do you have a spare tyre?" I ask, wrapping the blanket around me tighter.

"Yeah, in the back, but I've never had to use it," he stresses.

"I know how to change a tyre." I open the door, trying to ignore how cold I am. The sooner this tyre is changed, the better. I head into his boot and grab the necessary tools. I am lucky enough to find some gloves. My fingers are becoming numb, so I don't hesitate to put them on, and get to work.

"How did you become so good at changing a tyre?" Justin shouts over the wind, leaning over me.

"I always had cheap cars which were never reliable. You quickly learn how to fix it yourself, or things become very expensive, very quickly." Icy droplets get into my eyes, and I reaffirm my opinion that I hate snow.

I finish changing the tyre, and practically run back into the car, and wrap the blanket around me. My hair is wet from where the snow had settled on my head. Looking in the mirror, I see my cheeks and nose are red, and my eyes are watering from the cold.

"I'm impressed. That took you no time at all," Justin praises, turning the engine on and setting the heating on full. I don't say anything as my teeth chatter, but I nod and give him a shivering thumbs up before I retreat my hand back into the warmth of the blanket.

"I'll get you back and into the warmth," he says, rejoining the road.

After a few more minutes, I look out of the window as we enter a little village. It has idyllic old cottages, covered in thick, white sheets of glistening snow. The road is cobbled and extremely narrow. I'm not a stranger to narrow roads in Wales, but this road isn't one way. If anyone drives down this road, they will have to hope not to see anyone else, or it will mean a very long reverse job.

Each house has a gigantic wreath hiding half of the front door. Each one is bigger than the next, like the neighbours are competing. We drive by a lake which has frozen over. The more houses we drive past, the more Christmas decorations they have up. Some cover everything, from the house all the way to the mailbox.

Justin takes a left and stops in front of a gigantic gate. He opens the window, and the howling wind pierces my ears as it fills the car with snow. I had only just warmed up!

He quickly presses a few buttons, and the gate opens.

Wow, fancy.

He starts the car again and drives up to a considerably sized house. In fact, there isn't an adjective grand enough to describe how big this house is. Gigantic, massive, humongous aren't good enough. This house is the house that all kids dream of growing up in.

I can see a balcony which is wrapped in Christmas lights, as if it is a Christmas tree. There are tall columns and arched windows at least twenty feet high. As the car is parked, I can see a pond poking out from behind the house. It is, of course, frozen.

I can't help but observe the thousands of Christmas decorations surrounding the property. They have twinkling lights on everything you can imagine. They are covering the trees, and even the plant pots didn't escape untouched.

It can confirm it actually does look like Christmas threw up all over their house. They must be a Christmas loving family, which is just *so* amazing for me.

"This is where you live?" I ask, not taking my eyes off the house. It is huge.

"Yeah, my living quarters are near the back of the house. It's not big, but it's enough to get some privacy away from my family... They can be a bit much sometimes."

"Wow, back up. Do you actually have your own *living quarters*?"

"I understand that makes me sound incredibly pretentious, but yes. I have my own living quarters," he says, chuckling and taking the keys out of the ignition.

Wow, how much money do they have?

"Do you think you can make it to the house?" Looking out the window, the snow is still coming down hard. The tyre tracks Justin has just made with his car vanish. It is treacherous out here.

"Well, we don't really have a choice. I don't want to be snowed in a car with little heating." Justin takes that as a sign and flings the door open. Snow blows in and I squeal. Not wanting to stay here anymore, I open my door, accepting the fact I will freeze and snow may continue to get into some uncomfortable places.

I follow Justin to the front door. I will have to raise my arm to reach for the handle, it's that big. I don't think I've ever seen a house quite like this one.

Justin and I go through the doors, and are welcomed with blissful warmth. It hits me immediately, and my limbs tingle as they regain their feeling. I almost moan at how exquisite it feels. My cheeks are burning and my eyes are watering. Unwrapping my scarf, I pull off my gloves and wiggle my fingers.

Once my body defrosts slightly, I look around and am welcomed by a grand staircase with two women beaming at me.

"This is my mother, Evelyn, and my sister, Rose"

Rose is the first one to rush towards me, giving me a tight hug. She is small, so she has to cling to me and go up on her tiptoes to reach my shoulders. I have to stop myself from cringing and pulling back, but I return the hug and give her a light smile. It is the best I could do. Rose is petite with blonde, spiky hair, and sapphire blue eyes. It must run in the family.

This is only three days and a lot of money. I repeat it over and over in my mind.

"It's so nice to meet you, Grace! I'm so excited you're here to capture this magical moment for me." She flashes her gigantic ring, wiggling her fingers. It has to be at least five carats. Maybe more, I'm not an expert in expensive-looking jewellery.

"I'm very excited and honoured you requested me, and may I say, that ring is gorgeous!" I have gotten very good at feigning excitement when I am really tired. She holds her hand closer for me to have a second look. I'm not really all that interested.

"Who and where is the lucky man?" I ask, trying to learn more about this family. The more I know in the beginning, the less conversation I need to make later on.

"His name is David, and he's just upstairs sorting things out for the party later on!" Looking at Justin's family, I can see they have been blessed with great genes. They are all gorgeous with their light brown, wavy hair, and their strong jawlines.

"Party?"

"It's not really a party, Rose" Justin shot his sister a small glare. "But yeah, I should've mentioned it in the car. It must have slipped my mind. We're having a small meal to celebrate David and Rose."

"What about the storm?" I ask. Surely it's not just going to be us.

"It's a family gathering, so everyone who is coming to the dinner is already here," he says.

"Which is where I should be but wanted to welcome you." Evelyn gushes, gently taking my hands in hers. When her hands touch mine, my shoulders relax as I feel calmer. Her kind, blue eyes welcome me, and I remember how it feels to have a mother's warm presence. Evelyn is also gorgeous with her long, blonde hair and perfect eyebrows.

"I just want to say thank you for coming on such short notice. I hope we're not ruining any of your Christmas plans." Justin glances at me as she says that. I smile, not sure what else to do or say. I am running out of material.

"It's honestly no trouble." I completely ignored the inquiry into my Christmas plans because I don't want to lie, but I also don't want it to be public knowledge that I'm not planning to spend Christmas with my family anyway.

I look around, and my eyes become glued to a gigantic tree.

They have completely decked it with multi-coloured lights with a wide selection of baubles. The only thing which impresses me is the fact no lights are out. There have to be at least a thousand lights and not one is broken.

"Beautiful, isn't it?" Evelyn is staring at the tree as her eyes gloss over with pride. Not wanting to offend, I make a small noise which I hope will suffice.

We all stand there staring at the tree for a minute before Evelyn claps her hands together, making me jump.

"Well, I better get back to the kitchen. Justin will show you to your room, so make yourself at home," she says and floats towards what I assume to be the direction of the kitchen.

Justin picks up my bags and the coat that has fallen on the floor.

"Are you ready to follow me?" he asks, already making his way down the corridor. I would've thought my room was upstairs, but Justin walks straight past the stairs.

I say nothing as I follow him, giving his sister one last smile and wave. She returns them with more energy than I give and I have to admit, it is slightly endearing. She seems nice and she doesn't seem like one of those bitch brides I've encountered before. You never know with some brides.

As we walk through the house, I can't help but stare at the amazing structure. It is definitely an old house with touches of modernisation. The furniture inside is modern beside the odd coffee table or arm chair. There is a wall which is made entirely of stone with a fireplace underneath covered in stockings and a garland.

I walk down another hallway and through some double doors. Justin turns to me.

"These are my quarters. You have a room already ready for you here," he says and stops at a door. Even the bloody bedroom doors have a wreath and a bauble hanging from the doorknob.

"I'll just give you some privacy. I'll be in my room getting ready for dinner if you need me." He walks a few steps down the hall and opens the next door along.

"That's your room?"

"Yeah, come and knock whenever you need something." He gives me a smile and disappears into the room.

That's strange. I thought I was going to be next door to his sister or something. That would have made more sense, since she is going to be the focus of most of the photos.

I walk into the room, and of course, it's big. There were never any qualms in my mind about that and I was fully expecting a decorated room and I am, yet again, correct. There is a full sized Christmas tree in the room's corner with lights strung over the bed and down the walls. I have to admit; they impress me. The amount of thought and effort they've put in is incredible.

As I stand in this well-lit room, I can't help thinking about their electric bill. It must be through the roof.

I spend the next hour unpacking my things, getting my photography equipment charging and set up, and having a poke around the bedroom. It's like its own suite. No, scratch that, it is like a big apartment.

This entire house makes my apartment look like a flat pack doll's house. I can't resist having a snoop around my room.

I am nose deep in the drawers when I hear a knock on the door. I shut the drawer, trying to be quiet, but it slams.

"Shhhh," I whisper, not wanting anyone to know I am snooping. When I realise he will probably assume I just finished unpacking, I roll my eyes at my stupidity. I head over to the other side of the room and quickly open the door, Justin jumps slightly from where he stands in the hallway. I smile slightly in apology and take the opportunity to look him over.

CHAPTER FIVE

He's wearing a tinsel red blazer with black jeans, and he looks just as handsome as he did earlier.... minus the new Christmas jumper he has put on under the smart blazer. Not much has really changed at all, but he looks slightly different. Did he shave? No, it must be the blazer.

While I am pondering on what has changed with Justin in the last hour, he is staring at me with an arched eyebrow and the hint of a grin. I amuse him and that makes my stomach do a tiny flip, which I ignore. I am only here to work, I remind myself.

"Are you ready to come downstairs?"

No, but I don't have a choice. I just have to keep reminding myself, I am being paid quite a lot for this.

"Yes, I just have to get my camera." I'm not sure if I am supposed to be taking photos of the meal, or if they are wanting to wait until tomorrow. Either way, I am going to be prepared.

I go back into the room and say a brief prayer in my head that this would be a relatively normal family dinner, where I can just take their photos and leave. I have already noticed the wall mounted revolving drink dispenser, and I am definitely seeing this as a free bar.

I walk out of the room and stand with Justin in the corridor. He gestures for me to follow him down the hall and we walk side by side.

"How much of a struggle is this going to be since you hate... sorry, *dislike*, Christmas?" he questions. I scoff, wondering why he was asking a question so intrusive. Any way I respond to that question, I'll still sound awful.

"I'm just here to work, so I won't need to join in with any Christmas activities."

Justin laughs a full belly laugh, and I look at him with a raised eyebrow. Why is that funny?

"My mother will not rest until you've joined in. She has this thing where she desperately wants everyone to feel welcomed. You won't get out of it that easily," he says, still chuckling to himself.

"But I'm here to work so she'll probably un-derstand."

"Yeah, let's test that theory." His voice holds a certain challenge to it. A challenge I'm not sure I like because he sounds too confident in the outcome.

We walk into the kitchen, and the clatter of dishes, a pop of a bottle of champagne being opened, and beeping from the oven and microwave bombard me, but the loudest noise of all is coming from Evelyn.

"Now everyone, we are almost ready to put the stuffing in the oven, so be prepared. We need all hands on deck!" She is frantic. "No, that's not how you season veg!"

She hasn't seen me and Justin come in yet, but I am hoping she won't notice us for a few more minutes because this is hilarious to watch.

"Oh! Grace! I didn't see you there." I knew it wouldn't last long. "Sit down and the food should be ready soon," she ushers me out into the dining room.

"Are you sure? I don't mind helping or even shooting some pictures of you guys cooking together," I offer.

"No, you are a guest, it's your first day here, and you *will* relax. We have enough time for photos later and, besides, this isn't my best apron," she jokes, wink-ing. I fake a laugh and sit down, not wanting to drag this out any longer than needed.

Justin shoots me a knowing smirk from the kitchen as they force him to mash the potatoes. I smirk at him and watch as his eyebrows rise and his smirk grows bigger, clearly beating mine.

Well, what do I do now? I get up and look out through the window. You still can't see the road or the grass. It is at least seven inches. I have a few days for this snow to calm down, or else I face being stuck here.

"Grace." Rose comes into the dining room and sits at the table. She has changed into a green ombre dress with sparkling snowflake sequins running along the bottom. She looks dazzling as I ponder on whether I should change into something a little more formal. I am still wearing the jeans and jumper that I had travelled in.

She gestures for me to come and sit with her. Great, bonding.

"I was hoping we could discuss the photos for the wedding. I have so many ideas!" She pulls out a giant book which reads 'Wedding planning 101'. She heaves it onto the table with a thump and flicks to the tab labelled 'photos'.

I have to admit, this girl is methodical and precise. I can respect that.

"You're very organised," I acknowledge, raising my eyebrows at the diagrams and spreadsheets.

"Thank you! I try to stay organised," she says, clearing her throat.

"Or else she turns into a Bridezilla. Trust me, no one wants that after last week," David jokes, chuckling and flicking through the book's many pages. Rose shoots him a look.

"Yeah, we really don't want that." Another man walks in, a man I have not been introduced to yet. Rose jumps up, wraps her arms around his neck, and kisses him as if they were alone in the room. Ah, so he must be the fiancé. Or at least, I hope so.

I stand up and offer my hand as I clear my throat, causing them to break apart. He looks dishevelled, and I hide a smile as he takes mine.

"I'm Grace, the photographer." His once glossed over eyes focus, and he shakes my hand, looking a little embarrassed. He has nothing to worry about, I have seen so much worse.

"I'm David, the fiancé." He has golden hair and a trimmed beard with ginger specks. He's tall and next to Rose, he looks like a mountain and I can't help but notice the contrast between them.

"It's nice to meet you, so tell me more about the Bridezilla moment." It's probably a good idea to find out what I could be dealing with over the next few days.

"I don't think so. It's very traumatic for me," Rose sniffles, covering her mouth. She sulks into her book, mumbling to herself as David and I chuckle.

"Let's just say, the flower arranger can't handle another angry phone call," David mutters, shooting Rose a joking smile.

"In my defence, every bride has to be a Bridezilla at least once in their wedding journey, and it hasn't happened since! Not since I designed this book, anyway. It's Bridezilla proof."

"Tell me about your plans for the photos." I can already imagine how outrageous her demands are. I bet she wants angel wings, attached to strings, and she is lifted into the air and on top of a giant Christmas tree. It happens. Specifically, it happened at a shoot I did about two years ago.

"I want some casual photos, especially with my nan and the family where we are eating dinner or watching movies. It sounds stupid, but I would love to have a few with them before…" she trails off, and I remember what Justin had said in the email. Their grandmother is ill, and it is terminal. Crap.

David gently takes one of Rose's hands in his and she wipes a small tear from her eyes.

"I'm sorry to hear about your grandmother, and I'll do everything I can to capture every magical moment with her in the three days I'm here." I am truly sincere. I know what losing someone is like, and I wish it on no one.

She sniffles, but straightens her back and forces a smile.

"Thank you, Grace." She swiftly moves on. "I have an idea that I would love to do. I have vision boards in this book." I don't even have to ask to see them. She is already flicking through the pages and pointing them out to me.

"I want a white, snowy, magical photoshoot with romantic, white Christmas lights with mistletoe above us whilst we kiss."

Listening to her idea, I am impressed. It isn't too much that I would struggle with, it's classy and something I am definitely excited to do... minus the Christmas side of it.

"Sounds perfect! Where were you thinking of doing it?"

"I was hoping to go to the place we first met but because of the snow, I don't think that's possible." She looks out the window and her eyes lose some of their shine. I think it is a bit cliche to take a photo where you first meet, but if it is important to her, it is important to me as the photographer.

"I'm sure I can make your garden look like the place you met. Where was it?"

"It was at the cinema, actually. He was work-ing behind the tills, and I was there with a few friends about eight years ago. My friends and I bought a late night ticket and when the film finished, the cinema was just about closing. It was pouring down with rain, and I was the only one who didn't bring a jacket. He came outside, took his jacket off, and gave it to me despite the fact he would end up soaked!" she giggles. She looks up at him with so much love in her eyes, and he returns the look with just as much passion. They are glowing and at that moment, I see how this happened. They have so much love for each other, and I can feel their connection. Something pangs in my chest and I'm not sure what it is, but I don't think I like it.

"That's a beautiful story," I say, truly meaning it despite the feeling I had a few seconds prior. I distract myself with all the ideas I have to make this photoshoot perfect for them, and I'm beginning to think that the next few days won't be as bad as I thought.

This is why I became a photographer. I love the excitement of a new idea coming to life and seeing my client's face light up when they see how it turns out. It is my passion, whether I like Christmas or not.

"So do you have any ideas about how we could incorporate how we first met into the shoot?" she asks, with hope filling her eyes.

"I have a few ideas, yes," I smile, ideas flying around in my head.

"Oh, tell me!" she exclaims, sitting up from her chair and clapping her hands. David watches with adoration in his eyes and I know David has his own ideas, but is putting them aside to make her happy. He will do whatever he can to ensure she is happy. That strange pang happens again.

"You have everything else figured out. Let me surprise you. I promise it will be good and that you'll love it," I say. She looks at David and then back at me.

"Okay, sounds exciting!" She beams from head to toe.

"Great! I'll get to work immediately."

Evelyn comes in and tuts.

"Nope, we will do no work until *after* dinner. We will eat, talk, and enjoy ourselves before the proper work begins," she says, handing me a napkin. I place it on my lap, knowing how messy I am. She tells David to dish up and Rose to help set up the table while she fetches her 'good' china, and I am left alone. I lean back in my chair, happy for a few minutes of peace.

Justin pokes his head around the door, signalling for me with a panicked expression. Whatever this is, it definitely intrigues me, and I am out of my chair without a second's thought.

I follow Justin into the kitchen. He stands looking at giant Yorkshire puddings and a massive bowl of mash potato, scratching his head.

"Everything okay? Can I help in any way?"

"I hope so, otherwise I'm dead." His voice is frantic as he stares down at the mash potato.

"Should I even ask?"

"My ring is in one of these." I laugh in disbelief. He looks at me, his eyes wide, as if he can't believe I am laughing.

"Don't laugh. You don't know how crazy my mother is about not wearing rings when preparing food. She always goes on about it and I always thought it was nonsense." He stares at the food again, and I am bursting at the seams with laughter. He rolls his eyes and waves his hand at me.

"If you won't be serious, I will sort this out myself."

"Oh, come on, admit it, it's kind of funny. This would be a hit in a comedy!" I say, making my way over to the Yorkshires.

"I'll think it's funny once we find the ring and I keep my balls," he mutters, making me laugh even harder.

I look at the food and put my hands on my hips, instantly deciding that I wouldn't be going near the bowl of mash potato.

"You take the mash, I'll take the Yorkshires."

"I think it would be better if you feel around the Yorkshires and I'll wait until I know there's nothing in them before I stick my hands in that," he says, grimacing at the steaming bowl in front of him.

"Fine, but if they're not in here, you're putting your hands in that." He sighs but agrees because he has little option here.

I get to work, picking up a hot Yorkshire pudding and feeling around to see if I can feel anything hard which resembles a ring. So far, I feel nothing and my hands are on fire.

For a moment, I wonder what ring it is. Is Justin married and no one has mentioned it yet?

"Will your wife be annoyed once you tell her you've lost your ring?" I try to casually fish for some answers. I'm not sure why I care but I can't stop myself from asking. I distract myself from his inevitable answer by feeling more boiling hot Yorkshire puddings.

"What?" he asks, confused. "Oh, I'm not married. The ring was my grandfather's. It's been in the family for generations."

"Was? Is he not with you anymore?" I ask, trying to be careful. Last thing I want is to upset him, especially since his grandmother is ill.

"No, he's still with us. He gave it to me when I turned eighteen. It's been in our family for decades, and this is the first time it's been off my finger." I can't help but grimace. If we find it in the Yorkshire pudding or the mash, I'll know which one to avoid later, although having our hands in the middle of each bowl isn't particularly appetising either.

"So where is he?" I still have a few family members to meet, so perhaps he is somewhere in the house.

"He's upstairs with my grandmother. They'll be down for dinner soon. So what about you? What's your story?" he asks, leaning against the counter while I poke more Yorkshire puddings.

"You know my story. I'm a photographer who dislikes Christmas, and I'm photographing a family over the Christmas period." I didn't really want to reveal too much.

"Yeah, I know that." He flashes a playful smirk. "But what about your family? Are they still around?" he asks, and I squirm.

"I lost my mother when I was fourteen." I reveal, and he straightens. I purposefully avoid eye contact with him as I feel around the last Yorkshire.

"I'm sorry to hear that."

"It was a long time ago."

"What about your dad?" he asks, folding his arms.

"My father still lives in Wales with his new family." I try to keep the animosity out of my voice, but from his expression, I fail.

"Something tells me you're not happy about that," he leans against the counter, no longer interested in his ring. I scoff, avoiding his, what I know will be, judgmental gaze.

"Are you going to help me look for the ring, or not? Your mother will be down any minute and then you're screwed," I say, a little too harshly. I'm not even sure why I snap when it comes to my family, because I'm sure everyone has a family they're not entirely pleased with. No one is perfect, so what bothers me about mine?

Justin looks at me with a knowing gaze, so I try to deflect the tension with some comedy.

"Also, if we don't find this ring, I guarantee I'll be the one who swallows it and chokes. That's just my luck!" I say, nervously laughing. I think Justin can see this was a sore topic for me and leaves it. Thank the heavens. This is not something I discuss with my client's. I think it's very unprofessional.

"I don't think it's in the Yorkshires…" He stares at the bowl of mash, his eyebrows pulled down and his nose wrinkled in disgust.

Putting my hand to my mouth, I grimace and wash the oil from the Yorkshires off. I attempt to stop the laugh which threatens to spill out of my mouth. He didn't laugh at me...much, so I technically shouldn't laugh at him.

"Here I go." He holds his hand out and slowly puts it into the mash, grimacing as he touches it.

"It's rather hot and incredibly disgusting. I won't lie," he grimaces, cautiously adding his second hand to the bowl.

"If you're serving up the food, I'll kindly request not having the mash." He annoyingly mimics me.

"My hands are clean! I'll give you double servings of my hand-mashed potato." I crinkle my nose and shake my head after taking a minute to think about his absurd promise.

"I think I'm good. I won't be having the mash tonight," I fold my arms and squint my eyes, waiting for him to challenge me. He raises his eyebrows, a small smirk forming on his lips, before he quickly takes one hand out of the mash and presses his hand to my cheek. Gasping, I slap his hand away and wipe my cheek with my sleeve.

He did not just do that.

"You did not just do that!" Some of the mash has fallen inside the front of my jumper. I shake it, hoping the clump of mash will fall out before it works its way into my favourite bra.

Justin laughs and flashes the ring in his mash-covered hand.

"You found your ring! I would be happier about it if you hadn't ruined my favourite bra though." He cocks an eyebrow, and I roll my eyes.

"Justin, what's taking so long? You should've dished up by now!" Evelyn rushes into the kitchen, and heads straight for the vegetables in front of me.

"We didn't mash the potatoes enough, so I took it upon myself to sort that out," he says. Evelyn raises her eyebrows, tutting. Justin quickly thinks up another excuse. "I was also talking to Grace. You know, making her feel welcome."

Her eyes instantly light up "You're a good boy," she says, giving his hand a light pat. She grimaces at the mash on her hand, grabbing a nearby towel. "And clean yourself up. We have guests," she scolds, before she glides out of the kitchen balancing three plates full of food in her hands.

Justin and I share a quick look, and I know he is thinking the same as me. She didn't even question the mash on Justin's hands.

We smirk at each other before we grab a few plates and go to the dining room to help dish out. The table is now full of delicious food. I hadn't even realised how hungry I was until I looked at all the food on the table. There is every vegetable you could think of, even brussel sprouts, which no one really enjoys but forces themselves to eat at Christmas. There is beef, chicken, turkey, even gammon and pigs in blankets. Is this a Christmas dinner?

"Do you have Christmas dinner early?" I ask, taking my seat. Evelyn has written up name cards for everyone. It didn't surprise me.

"No, dear, whenever we have a cooked dinner, we like to go all out. We love a roast dinner in this house." Evelyn places the sauces in the middle of the table. They have mint, apple, cranberry, and horseradish. I am literally in sauce heaven.

"Can I stay with you more often?" I joke. Everyone laughs as they take their seats, and murmurs their acceptance to my proposal. Looking around, there are a few empty chairs left. I'm assuming they are for their grandparents. Potentially Justin's father?

"Who else will join us?" Just as I ask, a man walks into the dining room, holding a frail-looking woman close to him, so she won't fall down. The woman has a bright shawl hanging from her shoulders, and a ribbon running through her silver locks. The man holding her wore a navy country cap, and a flannel waistcoat. They were clinging to each other, as Justin and David immediately got up from their seats and helped the man.

I'm guessing these are Justin's grandparents. I stand up from my seat, waiting to introduce myself.

Once Justin's grandmother is sitting in her chair safely, I walk towards her and extend my hand.

"I'm Grace, the photographer, it's so nice to meet you." She smiles a huge smile and takes my hand. For a woman who needs help walking, she sure has a firm grip.

"Marilyn." That is a gorgeous name, and before I can say so, she speaks again. "You're a beautiful woman. I bet you get all the boys." She winks, and I blush.

"Oh, no, I don't think so. In fact, I think I'm cursed!" I try to turn this entire situation into a joke, and deflect from my disappointing love life. Everyone looks at me chuckling, intrigued by our conversation.

Why does everyone in a relationship feel the need to ask that sort of question? I know she means nothing by it, but shouldn't they know it's no longer polite to ask such a question? Especially to someone they've just met. It would certainly be rude if I took the same approach with her.

I can just imagine it, me asking how her marriage is going. I think that question holds an equal amount of rudeness.

"A good-looking girl like you should have a long list of fellas! Trust me, beauty doesn't last long and your clock is ticking," she insists, placing her napkin on her lap. Justin chokes on his water, and Rose gasps. I cringe so hard. Again, I know she isn't trying to be rude, so I ignore the comment and try to change the subject. I look at Justin's grandfather and hold out my hand.

"Grace," I say, my cheeks burning as he looks at me with an apologetic glance.

"Arthur." He shakes my hand and pulls me in gently. "You never get used to them." I hold back a chuckle as he pats my hand and walks towards his seat.

Another, younger, man comes in and gives Justin's mother a kiss. It goes on for a little longer than the rest of the people around the table like.

"Jesus, George. We have a guest," Arthur scolds, spooning some roast potatoes onto my plate. I put my hand to my mouth, holding in a laugh. This guy is hilarious, and he is definitely going to make these three days enjoyable.

"I'm sure she'll understand. After all, love is precious," George replies, sitting beside Evelyn.

"She hasn't got a fella," Marilyn mutters. Oh my God. Actually kill me now. Maybe if I walk in the storm long enough, I'll freeze over and forget this entire conversation.

George looks up, surprised. Gosh, it is like any woman in her mid-twenties must have a partner. If they're not married with kids, they are too career-focused or have something missing from their lives. Yes, I am dedicated to my career, but men never stick long enough for me. They are needy and often creepy; at least in my experience.

"Good God! When I was your age, I was married with a kid and another on the way!" he exclaims, taking a swig of his drink. I look down, feeling my cheeks getting redder.

I open my mouth to defend myself or say a joke to change the subject, but Justin speaks before I can form the words.

"Guys, you're being awfully rude. She's a guest, and this is not how our family treats a guest," he says, a very firm look on his face. I sit there, unsure of what I should do or say. I am both shocked and happy that I don't have to be the one to say how uncomfortable this conversation makes me.

His family bow their heads, muttering their apologies. Next to them, his sister, Rose, who didn't say a word, just eats her mash. She would not want to know that her brother's hands had been in that. Some things

56

are best left unsaid. A lesson which had to be learned today, apparently.

"Sorry, Grace. I understand that it's the modern day where most women aren't meeting anyone until their thirties, sometimes later!" Evelyn claims. Justin rolls his eyes at the pitiful apology, but I accept it. They don't have to mean it, as long as the topic isn't brought up again. Some people are just stuck in their ways, and that is fine. As long as I am okay with the way I live my life, I am happy. Mostly.

"No, it's fine. I'm happy and that's the most important thing," I say, trying to shut off the entire topic. It works.

"Well, tuck in. My wonderful wife has made enough for an army!" George says. Everyone obeys, thankful for the distraction as plates clanged and we passed dishes over and fell into friendly conversation. They ask how I got into photography and if I enjoy it. Of course I say how much I love it and explain that it is because I love seeing my ideas come to life through an image. It is always a magical moment when I snap a picture and my vision is there, in front of my eyes.

When we have finished cleaning up, I excuse myself for the night.

"You're going so soon?" Evelyn asks, putting the last plate back into the cupboards.

"Yeah, I want to make a start on planning the photos, especially since some ideas are so fresh in my mind," I say, just wanting to go into my room and have a drink with the optics. I have run out of social energy for one night.

"Okay, if you need any help, you know where to find me... or at least Justin. I've written everyone's phone numbers on a notepad in your room. It's right next to the phone, so if you have questions, just give one of us a call and I'm sure we can help you." Occasionally, she reminds me of my mother. They were completely different and had barely anything in common, but they both shared one thing. A mother's care. A few times when she is talking, I get the feeling of being safe and looked after. I only ever had that feeling with my mother, and it is strange to feel it again after so long.

"Okay, thank you. That actually helps a lot," I say, rubbing my arms. The snow is still falling, but it has eased since this afternoon. I am hoping it will continue to ease off for the duration of my trip, but nothing ever seems to go my way.

CHAPTER SIX

I walk into my room with a sigh and press my back against the door, as I truly feel how tired I am. My shoulders are stiff from all of the travelling, my face is aching from the fake smiles, and my eyes are incredibly sore from the bombardment of Christmas lights. This family, even though they seem nice, are overwhelming. They are a proper family, and I haven't been part of that kind of dynamic since my mother died. In some ways I miss it, but at other times I am happy being alone.

I wouldn't have had anyone to stick around if it wasn't for my best friend, Jasper. When I lost my mum, I lost nearly all of my friends too. Not through any fault of theirs, but through mine. I couldn't bring myself to talk to anyone. But then Jasper joined my school and sat next to me and he stuck. It took a while before I couldn't hold back my laughter with him. It didn't matter how horrible or miserable I was, he still stuck around and saved me a seat in the dinner hall. On that note, I owe him a phone call. I grab my phone and dial his number, letting myself get excited at the prospect of talking to him. I haven't spoken to Jasper properly in almost a week, and that is like an eternity for us. He has a new job, so it ties him up and I am in... well, in England. It's hard to update someone when you're travelling at the last minute.

He picks up after the third ring with his usual, "Hey Holly-day." It is the name he assigned to me the day we met. He said 'Your name reminds me of holidays in sunny places where I'm sitting on the beach getting sand in places where sand shouldn't be.' And that stuck with me because everyone associated my name with Christmas. The holiday I didn't enjoy at all.

"You still calling me that after all these years?" I say, not being able to hold back my laugh.

"Nope, it's stuck, I'm afraid." He sounds as if he is getting off a bus or a train.

"Like you, then?" I responded, sitting on the padded window bench in the room, looking out onto the frosty, snowy driveway. He laughs but doesn't deny it.

"Where are you anyway? Sounds busy." I can hear cars beeping and people laughing, with children crying and dogs barking. It is noisy at this time of night.

"I've just gotten off the train. Just heading into the centre to do some shopping if you want to join me? I was actually just about to head to your place and drag you out, kicking and screaming," he says, slightly shouting so I can hear him over the noise. During the Christmas period, the train station is always crammed with late night shoppers, frantically trying to finish their gift buying at the last minute. Again, I don't see the pleasure of this holiday. It just seems like everyone is stressed beyond breaking point, skint and having to deal with their miserable family members. Why is that fun?

"I thought there was a storm?"

"There is. There's talk of them cancelling all the trains tomorrow after a weather warning earlier today. I was hoping to get some last-minute shopping done before then because who knows when it's going to reopen?" Ah. That isn't the best news.

"Are you coming? You can buy me a super expensive present."

"I actually called to talk to you about that."

"Let me guess, you're not coming Christmas shopping because you hate all things Christmas and you'll die if you do anything remotely festive?" I roll my eyes. He is the only one who can talk to me like that. Everyone else would get an earful, joke or not.

"You're still not funny, even after all these years!" I click my tongue, trying to mock him, but nothing ever phases Jasper. It used to annoy me, but now I appreciate it.

"I know you're lying." He doesn't even try to hide the cockiness in his voice and before I can throw something back at him, he says, "So, what did you want to say?"

"I'm kind of... in England." I just rip the bandage straight off. Usually, when you tell someone shocking news, you expect them to be quiet for a bit. To digest the news and potentially think of a response. Like my dad did when I broke the news to him. But Jasper always has to be different.

He lets out a loud, ringing laugh. I hold the phone away from my ear until he is done.

"You're not joking, are you?" he says, realising I'm not joking when I didn't laugh with him.

"Nope, I arrived this afternoon. I was asked to do a photoshoot for this family for the next three days."

"Holly, you realise there's a storm?" Disbelief laces through his words.

"Yeah, and you've gone for a day out in Cardiff." What is his point?

"Cardiff is a lot closer than England! At least if I'm stuck in Cardiff, there's still hope for me to get home. If they cancel the trains, you're stuck with that family for the holidays," he says, and for the first time in years, he sounds worried.

"Jasper, I'll be back in three days. I doubt a storm will keep me out of Wales." The thought that I'll be stuck here is stupid. (I ignored the fact that the same worry had lingered in the back of my mind ever since I got here). People in the UK just seem to panic at the first sight of snow and rain.

"Holly, I don't know if you've thought this through...I know you don't like to spend the holidays with your family, but you always have me to go to. My door is always open for you," he promises, his voice soft and meaningful. Of course I know his door is always open, but this seems like something I *have* to do. If I hadn't come here, I just know I would have regretted it.

"Jasper, it's just something I had to do. Accommodation and travel were free and I'm being paid well to take a few photos of this girl's engagement. Easiest two grand I've ever made." He sounds like he choked on something. Maybe coffee? He is always drinking that awful stuff. I hate it. Tastes like sawdust and rust to me.

"Grand? Jesus, you should've let me come as your assistant and I could've taken a cut!" he exclaims. I can't help but laugh at the memories that brings up. When I was first starting out, Jasper would come with me to a shoot because I was nervous and anxious. We said he was my assistant or second-shooter, but really he was only there to support me and for the free food. He also enjoyed flirting with women there, which made my job harder at times, but I appreciate the sentiment. He stopped going when I was more confident and he was focusing more on getting a new job.

I miss him coming with me, but I know he has a life. Although I know if I do need him, he will be there.

"Oh yeah, and what would your job say about that?" I ask, truly enjoying his company.

"Probably, 'what an amazing and kind person, supporting your friend like that. We see you as a hero. Here's a pay rise.'" I laugh.

"Yeah, and I'm the Queen of England."

"Well, just be careful, Holly-day," he says.

We carry on talking for a few more minutes before he has to go into a shop. When we hang up, I feel lighter and motivated as ideas pour out of me. I jump off the window bench and head straight over to my photography book. It is a notebook I use to jot down all of my shoot ideas. I don't organise it to the extent of Rose's wedding planner, but it gets the job done.

Sitting on the bed, I pull out my empty pre-printed worksheets. It asks questions about every aspect of the shoot, from the venue to the props used and where I would find them. These worksheets are a lifesaver, and I print them in bulk. I can't be without them.

I fan them onto the bed, grabbing the first sheet. I start scribbling down the answers to the questions:

What was the theme of the shoot? Christmas wedding.

Where is the shoot being located? Back garden.

Describe your idea: Photoshoot in the back garden for Rose's wedding photos. A cinema set up with *blankets and comfy chairs, all under a canopy so they aren't covered in snow. This is to represent how they first met.*

As I am writing my idea down, I need a drink so I can finish this plan by tomorrow. I need all the help I can get.

Jumping off the bed, I make my way to the optics. It has a choice of whiskey, vodka, rum, and gin. The strawberry flavoured gin takes my fancy. That is my all-time favourite flavour, whether it is yogurt, ice cream, or an alcoholic drink.

I grab a glass and pour the gin, adding lemon-ade because tonic is disgusting and the worst thing to come from humans, and that is a pretty strong statement. It surprises me that they have both lemonade and tonic. Usually people only stock one. Not both. Either way, I'm thrilled.

Ambling back to the bed, I take a large swig and continue.

An hour later, I hit a problem. I'm not sure how I can incorporate their first meeting at the cinema outside when everything is covered in snow and ice. Last time I checked, snow was wet and things which are wet do not mix well with electronics. Crap.

Deciding to take a quick break, I head to the bathroom. There is an en-suite toilet, which I am very grateful for. I love not having to wander the halls, risking bumping into someone and having to engage in awkward conversation.

Heading back into the bedroom, I don't notice the corner of the TV stand and my leg smacks into it. I cry out and, as I bend down to cup my knee, I lose my balance and fall to the floor with a great thump, shouting out some very colourful words.

Suddenly, the door opens and Justin barges in looking quickly around the room, prepared for a fight. He scans the room until his eyes meet mine. Once he realises there is no danger, his eyes soften, and he comes striding towards me.

"I'm fine," I say, embarrassed and holding onto my throbbing knee. It feels warm, and I know there will be a large bruise on it tomorrow.

"Let me help you up," he insists. I shake my head and attempt to get up by myself. That fails as I stumble and hit my knee on the corner of the bed.

"Dammit!" I shout, feeling the humiliation of the moment just as harshly as the pain in my knee. It doesn't deserve this.

"Are you drunk?" he asked, smirking and gently taking me by the arm, helping me up. He encourages me to lean all of my weight on him as he carefully takes me to the bed.

"No, I'm not drunk. I've only had a couple of gins. I just didn't see the TV stand." I try not to fall over my words with embarrassment at Justin seeing me like this, a client. I think I have succeeded. Justin glances at the optics on the wall and definitely notices some of the gin is missing.

"Okay, let me at least get you a glass of water." He doesn't wait for me to reply. He grabs my glass and heads into the bathroom. I flop onto the bed, trying to sober up. I'm not drunk, but I can admit to myself that I'm not completely sober. I wasn't expecting to see anybody tonight, so I'd let myself relax.

Oh God, I bet I look awful. Still hearing the bathroom tap running, I jump up. Ignoring my stinging leg, I head for the mirror. It is as bad as I suspected. My hair is in disarray and my eyes are bloodshot. I didn't realise how tired I was. I quickly brush my fingers through my hair, annoyed at the kink that the snow had put in my once straightened hair. There is no hope for my eyes, and the joggers I had put on are also a lost cause.

Giving up, I limp back to the bed just in time. Justin comes back into the room, holding a full glass of water. I suddenly realise that my tongue feels like sand-paper in my mouth and I snatch the glass off him and gulp it down in seconds. I didn't know how thirsty I was until I saw it.

"Someone was thirsty." He chuckles and then his face turns serious. "You've cut yourself, Grace." He gets down on his knee and inspects my leg. I try to pull it away. I don't need him to fuss over me, I am fine. It is just a graze.

"I'm fine, it's not like I've broken it or any-thing." He sighs as if I am a difficult patient.

"Grace, just let me clean it. It's bleeding," he insists, still trying to examine my leg from where it is hiding behind my other leg.

I am seconds away from protesting again, but blood dribbles down my leg. It is then that I notice the bloodied patch on my joggers, so maybe it is a smart idea to just let him clean it. I do not want to lose a leg. I am the type of person to research why I'm sniffling and coughing only for Google to tell me I am dying. It makes me wonder what it would have to say about my legs, perhaps 'immediate amputation because of untreated infection'. Yeah, not today.

"Fine. But just so you know, I'm not drunk," I hear myself say it, and even I don't believe myself.

Justin doesn't reply, he just heads to the bathroom and opens the cabinet above the sink. From there, he pulls out a first aid kit. Huh, I didn't know that was in there. My snooping earlier had been interrupted, after all.

"Lay your leg on the bed and pull your trousers up to your knee," he instructs, opening up an antiseptic wipe. Normally I'd be annoyed at him for bossing me around, but I find that I don't mind too much right now..

"Yes, sir." I try to joke but he just raises his eyebrows and smirks at me. I'm not sure why, but my stomach flipped over at his expression. He kneels in front of me by the bed and dabs the wipe onto the cut. I hiss from the stinging pain which erupts from my leg and try swatting him away.

"Grace, it'll hurt for a second, but trust me, you'll feel better afterwards. Take it from a guy who has grazed many legs and broken many bones." That puts a small smile on my face because I can tell that he is trying to comfort me. It is not the most successful attempt, but at least he tried.

"What did you break?" I ask, trying to fill the silence, no longer able to listen to my groaning. I should be able to handle a few wipes. I am a grown woman, for God's sake.

"My right leg and both of my arms." He is still so focused on my leg, occasionally glancing up at me. I almost blush...I have to get a grip.

"Wow, that's a lot of big breaks. How did you break them?"

"I was playing football when I was in primary school, and my foot got caught on the net. I tripped and landed on both of my arms, because I was trying to soften the fall. My leg became twisted in the net and broke in a few different places, and my arms shattered. It was not a fun day for me, I'll tell you that."

"That sounds horrible! Did it hurt a lot?" I ask, completely forgetting about the pain in my leg. He looks up at me and raises his eyebrows before pulling out a plaster.

"You've never broken a bone before?" He asks it as a question, but we both know it is rhetorical. He is excellent at connecting the dots.

"Nope, I have never broken a bone in my body. I haven't even dislocated anything, either." I am always so proud of that fact. I am one of the clumsiest people I know, yet I am the only one in my family who has never broken a bone. My mother always told me it was because I was born with strong bones.

"Then you're very lucky. It was incredibly painful. I could barely move around for months." He finishes cleaning up my leg and adding a plaster, so I push my joggers back down and sit up.

"I don't think it's that lucky." He raises his eyebrow again, waiting for my explanation. "If or when I ever break a bone, I think it'll feel and be a lot worse for me because it never happened as a child. I'm pretty sure your bones are softer when you're a child?"

"I think so, but I also think a break is a break. Either way, it hurts like a bitch." He shuts the first aid kit and puts it back in the bathroom cabinet. "Actually, scrap what I just said. The worst thing about breaking a bone is the itching the cast gives you. It's never-ending, and you can never reach it. It's a highly effecting form of torture if you ask me." We both laugh as Justin walks over to the bed and sits down next to me. He looks behind me at all the papers fanned out.

"What have you been up to? Looks like you've been busy." He continues scanning the sheets, picking one up and giving it a read.

"I've been planning your sister's engagement photoshoot." He places the paper back down on the bed and looks at me. He looks so interested, like he really wants to ask me questions and find out about my planning process. Then, just as the thought came into my mind, a new one takes its place. Maybe he is interested because it is his sister's wedding, not because he was interested in how I plan or anything about me. Of course that is the reason.

"What have you got so far?" I'm sobering up the longer the conversation goes on. The glass of water I had guzzled, the pain from my leg, and the approaching conversation that looked to be about my favourite topic, photography, were all working together to get the alcohol out of my system. Having someone interested in my work, and willing to ask questions about it is a nice change. Usually around this time of year, people are asking the obvious Christmas-related questions: 'Have you got a boyfriend this year?' 'How much did you earn this year?' 'How have you been since your mother died?'

I try my best to avoid those sorts of questions, but questions about my work and ideas are allowed. In fact, those questions are my favourite. I love sharing my passion with whoever wants to hear it.

"Rose said she met David at the cinema. She was a little upset that she couldn't do some of the shoot at the cinema because of the snow, so I suggested I bring it to her." His eyes light up at my idea, and he edges closer to me. I'm not sure he realises he's done it but I definitely notice it.

"That's incredible! I'm assuming you're going to recreate it in the garden?" he asks. I nod, but don't share his enthusiasm. He tilts his head, frowning.

"What's up?"

"It's nothing." He doesn't look convinced. "I just realised as I was planning... how do I recreate the cinema during the snow? A blizzard? The worst seen in twenty-three years!"

"I have a few ideas," he says, laughing at my complete disdain for the snow. I sit up, practically begging for his help.

"What's your idea?" I ask, bouncing on the bed, pleased to be getting assistance.

"Do it inside. You mentioned it yourself, it's the worst snowstorm in twenty-three years," he says, chuckling.

Ah, I didn't think of doing it inside. I guess I got so caught up in making it romantic in the snow, but inside will do nicely.

"We've got an old projector in a room full of boxes upstairs. The room would be big enough once it's cleared of the junk and Halloween decorations. Should take a day to set up if we have all hands on deck."

"Halloween decorations?"

"Yeah, they're not just Christmas fanatics." It honestly does not surprise me.

"Okay, I like that idea. We'll have to work with what we've got. Maybe some items in storage will be useful for the shoot?" I ask. I picked up one of my worksheets.

"Yeah, there is loads of stuff up there. I can't even remember what's in that room, it's been so long."

"Be ready to knock on my door in the morning. You can take me up to that room and we can get started," I say, ignoring his grimace when I said 'in the morning.'

"I'll make a list of everything we can use in that room and then we can get started with the cleaning and setting up! Be ready at seven." I can feel myself getting excited again. It's an incredible feeling when you get loads of ideas after hitting a roadblock. I can't write them down fast enough.

"Sounds like a plan. A very tiring plan, but a plan," he says, getting up from the bed.

"If we're ready tomorrow at seven, then I'm going to insist I hit the hay. You do not want to see me until I've had my beauty sleep."

"I'm guessing you're not a morning person?" He answers my question with a grunt on the way to the door. Before he opens it, he turns.

"Are you going to be okay?" he asks, all joking aside. I nod, and we stare at each other, neither of us looking away. I can feel my cheeks burning red under his gaze, but I can't look away. I pull on my sleeve, trying to distract myself from his sparkling, tranquil, ocean-strong eyes, and I fear if I stare for too long, I will drown in them. Would that be a bad way to go? He has the kind of face which stops you in your tracks when you are in a cafe grabbing a coffee or when you are on the bus and you see him standing at the bus stop with a book in his hands. His eyes can make you forget about these mundane tasks. The tasks you do everyday, and never look up because it's your daily pattern. He can break that pattern.

It's like he's waiting for me to tell him I wouldn't be okay and I need him to stay and look after me. For some odd reason, I want to say that, but I don't. I have only just met the guy, and knowing my record with men, he would be fun for a day and then become needy. I don't want that.

"I'll see you bright and early tomorrow?" He nods, giving me a small smile which doesn't quite reach his eyes. He turns and opens the door, and my thoughts are almost overwhelming. My mind is shouting for him to turn around and insist that he stay.

He gives me one more smile and mutters a goodnight before shutting the door.

CHAPTER SEVEN

I practically fling myself out of bed at the sound of my alarm, which is a first for me. I immediately regret it as my head begins to pound and my whole body is covered in goosebumps. It is freezing, and I am definitely a tad hungover.

I clutch my head with a groan and pick up my cosy, life-saving dressing gown. All I can think about is that I need water. My throat is parched, and my tongue is stuck to the roof of my mouth. I finally find half a glass of water on the nightstand and down it in no time at all. I could really do with some paracetamol, but since I don't have a clue where that is, I settle for another water and a hot shower.

Today is going to be hard work, but I'm still looking forward to it. I waste no time and jump in the shower, grateful for the warm water, which makes my toes tingle from the contrast in temperature.

After my shower, I throw on a cosy jumper, comfortable jeans and thick woollen socks. Justin and I are going to be spending a lot of time sorting that room out and setting up the cinema, so I need to be dressed for hard work in a cold room. I am hoping to get most of the preparations done today so that we can start the shoot tomorrow. If I can get away from doing anything festive, I will have a wonderful holiday while working and doing what I love. That's all I need to do. Survive and get through another crappy holiday.

I tie up my hair and give the wall connecting mine and Justin's room a knock to let him know I am ready and, if he isn't, to get a move on. Or at least, I hope that my knock conveyed that message.

I walk out of my room, and I almost crash into Justin who has his hand raised, about to knock on my door. I jump back, grasping at my chest, trying to slow my heart.

"You ready?" he asks, a small smile on his face. I walk past him, excited to get stuck in.

"Come on, we're-" I check my phone, "-almost early. Let's keep it up, shall we?" I say, walking down the corridor.

"Grace?" he calls from behind me.

"What?" I say, still walking. Do I have to do everything myself?

"The room is this way." Turning around, he is pointing in the opposite direction from where I'm headed. Okay, small, embarrassing setback, but I can still come back from this.

I turn around and walk towards him, not looking at his smug face as I pass him. See? I sure told him.

"How are you feeling after last night?" he asks, finally walking beside me.

"I feel fine." I don't really know what else to say. *'No, I feel like a bus has run me over and I'm seconds away from falling over again.'*

We walk in silence down the corridors and stairs, which are filled with lights and a variety of Christmas decorations, and it still surprises me to see so many.

Justin stops at a door and opens it.

I walk in ahead of Justin and see the potential immediately. It is a loft conversion with the roof dipped on both sides, connecting in the middle. There is a big white wall with several boxes stacked in the corner. On the other side of the wall, there is an enormous chest of drawers, and I can't help but wonder what will be in there. My curiosity is peaking, and I can feel that tingle of excitement in my fingers and toes as I itch to get stuck in. There are a few boxes in the middle of the room with some loose items scattered around, and straight away I can see things which could be used in my shoot. I have a good feeling that we will finish this today.

"What's your plan?" Justin asks, leaning against the door frame, watching me take in the room.

"I think we need to look through the boxes and make a 'keep' pile and a 'throw' away pile. I'm hoping that should only take an hour." Justin scoffs.

"An hour? I bet it'll be at least two or three." We share a glance and I begin to smirk; it's a challenge then.

"Well if you keep messing around by the door, we definitely won't be finished in an hour!" I say, picking up a box from the corner and setting it on the floor.

"Someone woke up on the wrong side of the bed." I roll my eyes and don't bother replying. I know he is joking, but I am definitely not in the mood for jokes today.

"Come on, let's just get started," I say, waiting for him to say yet another sarcastic comment, but he doesn't object, and grabs one of the heavier boxes. I sit down and begin emptying a box. I'm not entirely sure what some of the items are. This box is just full of things which aren't going to be useful for the shoot, so I pack it all back up and place it in the 'throw away' pile.

I open up a second box and can't contain my snort of laughter

"Are you serious?" I call out across the room. Justin's head peeks up above the stack of boxes and he gives me a questioning look.

"You have a box full of Christmas decorations," I say, not even attempting to hide my mockery. This family has a ton of decorations already up in the house. Why do they have more stored away?

"Did you run out of space or something?" I ask, picking up some lights and tinsel and seeing they were all in pristine condition.

Justin laughs. "It's some of the older decorations which my mother has replaced," he says, probably realising how silly this sounds.

"So what will you do with them?" I am trying to sound less judgemental, but surely no one loves Christmas as much as this family.

"I'm not sure. My mother usually decides and sometimes she gives them away to charities, but if she's keeping them, she may want to use them for something." I can't hold it in any longer. My disdain for the holidays has won against my moral judgement.

"So she can use it in her grotto?"

The moment I say it, I regret it. But Justin doesn't seem offended as he rolls his eyes and sits facing me with a small smile. I squirm, trying to avoid his gaze by staring at the tinsel. The hideous, tacky-looking tinsel.

"Why do you hate Christmas so much?" Oh, here we go again. I am fed up with having to fend off this question over and over.

I sigh. "Just because I don't follow the norm, does not mean I owe an explanation to you or anyone else who feels the need to ask," I say, diving my head into another box.

"I'm guessing you say that a lot?"

"What makes you say that?"

"Well, you said it like you've rehearsed a script. It was extremely monotone," he says, like he has me all figured out. This hangover is definitely not making it easier to deal with this situation.

"When you tell someone you aren't the biggest fan of Christmas, you're treated like you're weird, or someone who is boring," I say, in full ranting mode. Nothing is stopping me now. "I'm treated differently, and I thought being unique was celebrated, but apparently Christmas never made that list." Taking a deep breath, I realise how quickly I am talking.

He opens his mouth to say something and then shuts it again, scratching his head. We stay silent, and I'm glad, I don't want to get into all of this in the first place.

As I put the tinsel and lights back in the box and pick it up to place it in the put away pile, Justin claps his hands together, making me jump. I put my hand on my chest, looking at him as if he has lost his mind.

"We can use the Christmas decorations to decorate the room for the shoot." That idea is actually not bad, and he is now back in my good graces.

"Yes! That's exactly what we'll do." I'm happy he has abandoned his questions about my dislike of Christmas.

I pack up the decorations and place them in the 'keep' pile. So far, that is the only box in that pile. I am going to have to dig for those hidden treasures if I want to set up this cinema today. It isn't like I could go to the shop, because we are still stuck in the middle of a blizzard. A blizzard I hope will be gone in two days so I can go home and hide out in my apartment, recharging my social battery.

I open another box and begin the process all over again. This box has a bit of everything. There are speakers, keyboards, and tons of electronic items. I know I could one hundred percent use all of this.

"Hey, Justin, check it out." He stands up and leans over me, checking out the contents of the box. My breath hitches and my palms begin to sweat. My heart is beating so hard, I fear he can hear it. He is so close. So close I can smell his aftershave and feel the cotton of his jumper against my cheek as he scours the box's contents.

"We can definitely use this entire box," he says, leaning closer and picking up some items. I hold my breath as he leans closer to untangle some wires, causing him to reach past me. I can feel the heat from his arm through my jumper, and my heart is beating faster with every second he's there.

Finally, he untangles the wires and places them back into the box, a lot neater than they had originally been packed in. And finally, I can breathe again.

He picks up the box and places it into the 'keep' pile. As he does, I can't stop looking at him. Maybe it is the hangover.

"Have you found anything?" I ask, looking out of the window from my spot on the floor. It's still snowing, and the sky is whiter than I've ever seen it. I am trying to distract myself from whatever Justin is doing to me, not really understanding my reaction to him.

"Not really. I do have that old projector though." He walks to the other end of the room and picks up the projector. Again, I look out of the window trying to distract myself from the way his jumper tightens around his shoulders as he picks up the heavy boxes. It's torture.

He shows me the projector, and it is definitely not that old. It reminds me of the projectors we had at university, so it could only be a few years old, and it seems to be in perfect working order.

"That's definitely not old. It looks brand new, actually," I say, getting up to inspect. There isn't even a mark on it.

"It's two and a half years old." He says it like I should know that it's old. Rich people are a whole different breed, and that one comment definitely makes me feel poorer than I actually am. For me, old is when something is falling apart and just about stops working. It could be ten years old and still feel brand new to me.

"So it's old because it's almost two years old?" Again, I do not attempt to hide my judgemental tone.

"Yeah, we also don't really use it. It was for my father. He used to watch films with a few friends during his poker nights. We have not used it in over a year." Wow. They're so blasé about discarding possessions because money doesn't seem to be an issue for them. I wonder how nice it must be not having to worry where or when your next pay check is going to be.

"Okay, we'll put it in the keep pile."

He does as instructed and opens a second box.
I do the same, and we work in silence for a few minutes
before Justin finds it too difficult to stay quiet.

"Do you live with your family?" he asks, placing more old magazines and documents in the put aside
pile.

I roll my eyes, seriously not wanting to start
this again. Sighing loudly, I hope he will get the hint,
and say nothing. I can feel him stare intensely at the side
of my head, and I can see him waiting for an answer out
of the corner of my eye. No way will I give in that easily,
so he will wait a hell of a long time. I can ignore him all
day as I rummage through a box full of cushions and
blankets. We can use these items for the shoot, but they
could do with a wash. I get up and place them in the
keep pile before returning to my spot, still not saying a
word.

I open up another box which is full of photo
albums and picture frames.

"You really have your walls up, don't you?"
he asks. I'm in shock that he can ask such an intrusive
question. He knows nothing about me, and yet he is trying to find out as much as he can.

"You really enjoy asking personal questions,
don't you?" I prod, having to keep my temper in check
even though it is rising like a rumbling volcano, threatening to erupt.

"Touché." He scratches his chin, still rummaging through the boxes. "Although, I don't think asking
if you live with your family is a personal question. You
know I live here with my family, so I'm just trying to be
polite and ask about you and your life. I'm also interested in knowing about the girl who travelled to England
to stay with another family for three days over the holidays, and who hates... sorry, *dislikes* Christmas."

"You really want to get personal?" I ask,
showing him a photo album labelled 'Justin'. He sits up,

leaning against the wall behind him and watching me closely. I shudder under his gaze and chew on my lip.

"What do you want to know?" he asks, draping his arm on his knee, challenging me with his cheeky smile. I accept, because I never say no to a challenge.

"What was your childhood like?" I ask, flicking through the pictures. "You looked quite shy and sad when you were younger." From looking at this photo, I can see that something has changed in Justin so drastically, and I can't stop myself from wondering what happened.

I am betting he won't tell me a thing because he is just as closed off as I am. When he refuses to answer, I'll finally be able to ignore his invasive questions and not have to justify my silence.

"Kids in school bullied me as a child because my family seemed pretentious. I had no friends because they were jealous of the things I had and they didn't have, even though my parent's money had nothing to do with me," he reveals, and I instantly feel bad for asking. Unlike most people, I have no interest in learning people's deepest, darkest secrets because I don't want to invade their privacy. I don't want Justin to feel like he has anything to explain to me.

"It's fine, Justin. You don't have to keep going. Let's just finish sorting out this room." I am beginning to unpack some more boxes when he speaks.

"No, no, I want to tell you. It's good to talk about these kinds of things; terrible experiences are easier to handle when you share your emotions with the people around you," he says, and before I can object, he carries on.

"When I went to College and University, I had friends. During this time, I met a woman who seemed fond of me almost as soon as we had met. Not having had many life experiences, I was so happy to be liked and have so much attention - attention people denied me as a child - that I didn't see any issues with her or my new friends." He pauses, deep in thought.

"There were a lot of rumours about my girl-friend and my best friend hanging out when I wasn't there.I didn't think too much of it at first, in fact, I was pleased that they were getting on so well. But these rumours carried on for about three months and became more and more suspicious. They were spotted going into each other's dorms and getting coffee when she had told me she was working. She kept asking me to buy her expensive gifts, and I was turning her down a lot of the time. I shouldn't have to be buying things for my partner all the time to make them happy." He stands up and looks out of the window, his eyes glazed over as if he were picturing the scene in his head. I let him talk, a part of me feeling angry that anyone would treat him this way.

"It was like a part of me knew what she was up to and that's why I denied her so often. I finally gave in and bought her an expensive necklace that she had been asking for; I planned to surprise her with it. I went up to her place during the Christmas break to give her the present, and I found the two of them together. I doubt I have to go into detail with that part." He briefly laughs, but the sound is forced, as if the memory is still too painful.

"I found out that they were both using me for my money and when I wouldn't give them both what they wanted, they turned on me and found each other." He stops talking, and I sit there in stunned silence. I want to take back all the comments and judgement I had thrown at him and his family during my time here, but I know I can't. It was done, and I feel like I'm no better than those people in the story.

"How can you still love Christmas when such a terrible thing happened to you? Doesn't it remind you of it each year? The heartbreak and humiliation you felt?" I ask, truly wanting to hear his answer.

He looks at me from where he stands by the window, his eyes gentle and kind.

"Of course I can still love Christmas. Just because something terrible happened, doesn't mean that I should give up my love for the holiday entirely. It took me a while to realise it, but that was probably the best gift I could have gotten that year. I was given the opportunity to get rid of some awful people in my life and really take a look at what I wanted for my future. You need to be able to see both sides of a situation. Acknowledging the bad experiences helped me to move on with my life, but if I had ignored the good, I would have become bitter, cynical, and never allowed myself to enjoy my favourite holiday again."

It feels like he is speaking directly into the hole in my heart that had carved out a place there. I frown, not knowing what to say. Is he trying to say I've turned bitter and cynical? He doesn't know what happened to me that caused me to dislike Christmas, so he has no right to judge me. I try to calm myself down before I say anything. After all, he had just shared a very personal memory with me and it wouldn't be fair to snap at him.

"I'm sorry that happened to you," I'm not sure what else I can say.

"It's fine. I'm happier now than if I were still in that place. It's a situation I've come to see as a blessing." He says that last part while making strong eye contact with me. His eyes never waver from mine, and it leaves me wondering if I have become bitter. In my attempt to keep things private, maybe I've made a wall so high even I can't break through it.

Justin says nothing else as he goes back to his spot on the floor and begins opening up yet another box and rummaging through its contents. As I watch him, I start to become jealous. He wears his Christmas jumper with pride and he holds himself in a way I can only dream of. He is happy and confident and can talk about hard topics with little encouragement and, in that moment, I realise I want the same freedom.

"My mother died when I was fourteen. It happened near Christmas." That is all I can say. I don't need to say any more because when Justin holds his head up and looks at me, I can see his understanding fall into place. His eyes widen ever so slightly, his breath slows, and his mouth partially opens. He licks his lips, weighing his next words carefully.

"I'm so sorry to hear that. That must've been so hard," he says, coming to sit next to me. His hands twitch, and I wonder if he will place them in mine, but he doesn't. I press my lips tight and focus my eyes inward.

"Is that where you get your negativity from regarding Christmas?" he asks with such softness in his tone. It is as if he is approaching a wounded bird and he handles it with great care so that he won't scare it.

I don't trust my voice, so I resort to just nodding. He shuts his eyes briefly and takes a deep breath, and I know he can feel my hurt. He finally understands, and I feel a huge weight lift from my shoulders, just like he had said it would.

I want to shout, *'Finally! Finally, someone understands. I'm not alone or left to think I was crazy. Finally!'*

"I know you don't see it now, but you have your own life to live. Christmas and this time of year had nothing to do with her death," he says, again in a gentle voice. He speaks like he is afraid he will spook me, but at this moment, he could've said anything and I would still feel calm. It's like when you hide something for so long and it finally comes out and you're unsure of what you should do or think or feel.

"Enjoy your life, Grace." Upon hearing my middle name, I cringe, regretting not telling him my name is actually Holly, but I fear the lie is too deep now. I can't tell him my real name because it is embarrassing.

I have always hated my name because I associate it with Christmas and my mother, and everything that I wish was different.

"I don't think I'll ever enjoy this holiday. It holds too many painful memories," I say, turning to another box on my left and attempting to sort through the contents.

Justin gently grabs my hands and places them in his. His hands are warm and soft, and it leaves me wondering how I have gone so long without holding them. My hands fit perfectly in his and I look up, meeting his eyes. At first, he looks at me sternly, as if he is going to tell me off, but as our gazes lock, I can hear electricity crackling and the sound of our heartbeats synchronising, and I know I want to stay here forever.

"Grace," he whispers, his eyes flickering to my lips for a second. I see the look and the intent behind it, and at that moment, I want it to happen. I want him to lean closer and kiss me. What is happening to me right now?

"Tell me what happened to your mother. Maybe I can help you get past this? Let me help," he asks, his face pleading with me, desperate to help in any way he can.

My heart won't stop racing, but I'm surprised to find I like it. In fact, I feel as if I could explode.

I decide to tell Justin a little about what happened, purely because I want to. I am already addicted to this feeling, and I never want it to go away.

"I was in my Christmas show at school. I was on stage, ready to read my part in the Christmas story, and I looked out to see if my mother was there. She wasn't, and it annoyed me. I was angry. She had never missed a show in all my years at school. She made sure to be at every single one." I pause, as something wedges itself in my throat. "I did the entire show without her there, and the longer I stood on the stage and saw none of my family, the more angry I felt. I kept thinking, *'what could be more important than your own daughter's show?'"* Justin nods, taking a deep breath and maintaining eye contact. He doesn't judge me when I say I was angry and, for that, I am grateful. I always feel ashamed of the fact that I have been so angry. I should've realised something was wrong, but I didn't.

"I finished the show and my grandma was outside. She took me to her house, and that was when I knew something was wrong. Her phone kept ringing and each time she took the call upstairs and each time she came back, she would look sick. No matter how many times I asked about my parents, she would change the subject and distract me with snacks and films she knew I was excited about. She tried distracting me with everything a teenager would crave, but I knew something was wrong." I pause and Justin squeezes my hand tighter, urging me to continue. I take a deep breath and carry on. I am almost done, but the more I speak, the better I feel. I can feel the burden lifting from my shoulders.

"My father came home, and he sat me down and told me that my mother was in the hospital. She had collapsed and hadn't woken up. I went to visit her every day for a week, but she never woke up." As I finish speaking, my shoulders sag, and I exhale, letting go of the tension I had been carrying with me.

"I'm so sorry that happened to you, but you shouldn't allow it to change you," he says. I frown, not really knowing where he is going with this.

"Of course I changed. I lost my mother, and my life was never the same."

"What changed?" he asks, still digging. I scoff.

"What didn't change? My entire life changed. I lost friends, my mood hasn't been the same since, my love life has been practically non- existent. Not to mention my family life." As soon as those words leave my lips, I regret them. I only want to tell Justin about my mother passing so he would finally understand why I'm not a fan of Christmas. I had no intention of revealing to him that the rest of my life was in utter shambles.

"What about your family?"

"Nope, I'm not getting into that. You have enough from me," I say, moving away from him. The spell breaks, and we are back in the storage room. Justin clears his throat and sits back against some boxes. We are no longer touching, and I miss the warm contact.

I can see Justin is about to ask another personal question, so I try to interrupt and do a complete subject change.

"Should we test the projector to see if it works?" I ask, opening the last box. It is full of old beer glasses and bottles, and I look at Justin with a questioning stare.

"Yeah, I'll plug it in once the room is empty. And that's my father's. He had a phase of collecting beer bottles and glasses to make some kind of sculpture, but it seems to have been abandoned halfway through. He just shoved them in a box and placed them here," He crooks his fingers into air quotes, "in case he ever needed them."

He stands up and walks towards me. I don't dare look him in the eyes. I just continue rummaging around in the box, even though I have seen everything already.

"Grace." He stops beside me. I still don't look up.

"Yes?"

"You should enjoy Christmas. I know your mum would want you too." I spin around so fast, I almost fall into the boxes. He reaches his hand out to catch me, but I shrug him away.

"You didn't know her. How could you possibly know what she would want?" I snap. I take a deep breath, trying to calm myself. I know it isn't his fault and he's only trying to be kind. "Why are you so obsessed with me not liking Christmas?" He doesn't look phased by my bad temper, he looks interested instead as if an idea sparks in his mind.

"I bet I can make you fall in love with Christmas," he says, holding his hands up. His eyes hold the twinkle of a challenge, and I know I won't be able to resist a challenge, but this one is ridiculous.

"Excuse me?" I laugh, thinking believing this to be a joke.

"I'm being serious. I bet I can make you fall in love with Christmas by the time you go home."

"In two days? I seriously doubt it. There's no changing me. I've been this way since I was fourteen." I don't need someone to change me.

"If I don't make you fall in love with Christmas, I'll give you something. Whatever you want," he says, and it shocks me that I'm even considering it.

"Why is this so important to you?" I don't understand it. If anyone told me they hated Halloween or their birthday, I'd wonder why, but I wouldn't attempt to convince them otherwise. That's their choice, no one else's.

"Because Christmas is about warmth and happiness and even though it may be cliché, it still brings people together. It's a joy in life and I just want to help you regain that."

"If you can't make me love Christmas, then I want to be your family's photographer and if your family has any friends who need a shoot, you'll recommend me to them," I bargain, knowing he won't succeed. If I become their photographer, I'll get tons of business from high paying customers. That would sort me out for months and give me some time to revamp my business.

Justin pouts as he considers it and nods.

"Okay, you have yourself a deal." He holds out his hand, and I hesitate. Am I going to regret this decision? What things does this bet include? My plan when I first arrived was to avoid any Christmas festivities for as long as I could. Have I just agreed to walk straight into them?

"And what do you win if you succeed?" I ask.

"I'll let you know," he says, flashing me a devilish grin. I guess this couldn't hurt. I wanted more excitement and risk in my life.

"Deal." Putting my hand in his and giving it a firm shake, I have a terrible feeling that I'll regret this, but I am a very competitive person, and I am interested to see what he will do to try and convince me. I would also be lying if I say I think he is going to succeed. At the ripe age of twenty-three, I'm already set in my ways. At least I get a lifelong, well-paying client out of all of this. After all, I said that I'm coming here for business.

CHAPTER EIGHT

We have finished sorting out the room until it is an empty shell, full of potential and beauty. As I stand, leaning against the door while Justin and David set up the speakers, I imagine everything that I can do with this room. I imagine where the freshly ironed sheet will go and where the blankets and pillows will spread beautifully on the floor. I can see where I will put the Christmas lights, and I'm getting excited.

"What's next on your list?" David asks, as they both finish plugging things in and 'testing the sound levels' or whatever they said they were doing.

Checking my clipboard, I smirk. Finally, something I can do.

"I'll be sorting out the blankets, but we have to sort out the sheet and hang it on the wall. That, however, is a one-man job so, David, I assume you know where the ironing board is?" I ask, and I am greeted by a very annoyed glare.

"What? It's a very important job and I don't iron." It is true, I don't. Justin scoffs, and I ignore him. He is lucky I didn't give him that job.

"Isn't it supposed to be a shoot for me and Rose?" David asks, folding his arms over his chest.

"Exactly, and don't you want everything to be perfect for Rose?" I lean closer to him and whisper, "Also known as your own personal Bridezilla?" His eyes widen, and he gulps, grabs the sheet, and practically runs out of the room.

"You realise that the Bridezilla you're talking about is my sister?" Justin smiles a warm smile which reaches his eyes, and I have to force myself not to look him straight in the eyes for fear of me falling into them again like I did earlier. Now, with the bet in place, I need to win.

"So you know what I mean." I focus on checking off items on my to-do list. It is a pleasure of mine. I absolutely adore lists and being organised, perhaps not to the extent Rose does, but lists are definitely my thing. I can't function without one. There is something so satisfying about seeing your to-do list getting smaller and smaller.

"Okay, want to help me set up the floor? We need blankets, pillows, a small table and lights." I walk outside to where the boxes of everything we need are stacked against the wall.

Where is the box labelled blankets? I can't see it.

Justin walks behind me, getting closer with each step. I can feel him behind me as he inches closer until I feel his chest pressing against my back. My breathing completely stops, but my heart is still pounding. So strong I fear he will hear it.

He is so close as he presses himself tighter into my back. Biting my lip, I shut my eyes, enjoying the warmth his body is giving me before it is ripped away.

One minute he's there, pressing into me as I feel the most intense heat, and the next he disappears and I am cold. I turn around, blinking the haziness away, and my eyes focus on his. He is carrying the box with the blankets with a small smirk on his face.

"It was all the way up at the top, so I thought I'd grab it. Save you climbing up a ladder to get it," he says, a slight teasing tone to his voice. I am struggling to make eye contact as my cheeks flare. I'm speechless.

"Grace? Without a snarky remark? Whatever will I do?" he says, chuckling to himself. He knows exactly what he is doing, and I will not allow it.

"I've got to give you a fighting chance or else it isn't fair," I say, brushing past him and walking back into the room. Yeah, I can give him sass too.

"Enough playing around. We haven't got time. Put the box on the floor there."

"Yes, boss." He places the box on the floor and rips it open. I don't waste any time getting stuck in pulling out the blankets. His mother washed them while we were finishing up the room earlier and placed them in the box, neatly folded. I have to give it to her, she has perfect timing.

"I have a few sketches and picture boards to show you how it should look." Pulling my photography planning book from my bag, I pass the sketches to Justin, and he flicks through them, looking quite impressed. That thrills me, which I immediately tell myself is a completely normal and professional emotion to have about my employer liking my ideas..

"This is impressive, Grace. How long did it take you to do these?" he asks, evaluating the pictures closely.

"I did it all last night. It's amazing how much gin can motivate you." Justin laughs and tries to hand me the book.

"No, you keep it. I have it all in here." I tap the side of my head.

I start picking up the blankets and arranging them in a way that will come across well to the camera, but also in a way which will enable David and Rose to watch the film afterwards and share a romantic moment.

"Justin, can you grab a small table? If there is one?" I ask, once the blankets and pillows are down. He doesn't hesitate. I mutter a thanks before David comes in with a freshly ironed sheet.

"Ah, that's perfect! Let's hang it up," I say, helping him bring the sheet over to the wall.

Once that's done, I can see the room slowly coming together. I attempt to hop down from the chair, but I miss my step. My arms clamour wildly, searching for anything to grip onto, but I find nothing. I close my eyes tight, waiting for the inevitable impact. My descent to the floor is halted by what feels like bands of steel wrapping around my legs and shoulders. I open my eyes and red fabric is all I can see. I slowly look up to find Justin's face above mine, gazing down at me in concern.

"Are you alright?"

"I - I didn't even hear you come in," I stammer, mind blank from anything else to say.

"I came back to get you," Justin said, still holding on to me. My stomach grumbles, and I have to clamp my hand over it in a poor attempt at trying to silence it. It's at that moment we both realise that I'm still being held in his arms. He lowers my legs down to the floor and steadies me as I stand. There is a blush on my face and I can no longer make eye contact with him.

"So, what were you coming to get me for?" I ask, desperately trying to get rid of the tension between us.

"We're going to eat some food."

"What?"

"I'm taking you to get some food. Neither of us have eaten yet."

I look back at the unfinished room, hesitant on leaving. I have work to do. Opening my mouth to say just that, Justin interrupts me.

"Come on, you're starving," he says.

"What were you thinking?" I ask, almost drooling at the thought of food.

"You'll see," he says, making me extremely suspicious.

"David, can you finish hanging up the lights and positioning the tables?" Justin asks. David gives us a stern stare from where he's watching us from the corner of the room.

"Yeah, because I'm not hungry," he says sarcastically. I'm not sure why he is so snappy with us.

"You're more than welcome to grab a bite to eat, but the lights and the table shouldn't take long and we should only be there an hour. Maybe two," Justin suggests.

"Fine, I'll stay and do as much as I can, and then I'll go get ready for the shoot," he says, rolling his eyes.

"Thank you. All of my notes are on the chair. Check it out whenever you need to," I say, hoping he doesn't mess it up. I will not have Rose sulking on my first shoot with this family. Whatever we are eating, I am going to eat fast so I can get back and make sure the job is finished correctly.

David nods, and we waste no time in leaving him to it. Justin leads me down a corridor I don't recognise.

"Where are we going?" He looks back at me with a cheeky smile and winks.

"You're impatient, aren't you?" I scoff, folding my arms.

"No, I'm just not ecstatic at the thought of walking around the entire house in search of food. It's not my idea of fun." I pause, looking around at all the decorations lighting the way. "It feels like I'm in the North Pole and you're the elf showing me the way."

"You know you use humour to deflect from your issues," he states, casually strolling down the hall, not looking at me.

"That is not true. You don't know me." How dare he be so presumptuous?

"It's fine, we all cope in our own ways." Now I do not know what he is talking about. Is he talking about the story I had told him earlier?

I stop in my tracks, and he turns around, giving me a questioning look. He does not know what he is doing, does he?

"What are you talking about?"

"Just that you're very similar to myself. I see a lot of myself in you and I want you to realise that part of yourself."

"You sound like a preacher."

He laughs and stops at a door, opening it for me. I walk in and see the bright, clean, and organised kitchen. It's the kitchen of my dreams.

"I didn't even see this door yesterday." I can't believe I hadn't noticed it.

"In your defence, they've covered it in Christmas lights and a wreath, so I'm not surprised that you missed it." He walks me to the corner of the kitchen, where there is a small table. There is cutlery already arranged, and there are two glasses of red wine.

"What's this?" I ask, cautiously approaching the table. What is he up to? This can't be a date, so what does he want?

"It's part of the bet," he answers, pulling back my chair. I sit down and laugh.

"Really? You think some food and red wine are going to make me fall in love with Christmas?" I can't hide the mockery in my voice. If this is his grand plan, I am in for a very easy win and a new client soon.

"This is just the start, but yes. I have some ideas and I thought this was the best way to ease you in," he says, and I have to stop blushing. Maybe all the festivities have gotten to my head, and that is the reason I can't think straight. As Justin just said, there's a lot going on.

"Okay, I'll play along. Let's see what you've got"

"Excellent."

He walks to the oven and the food smells delicious. I inhale, trying to taste the food before he even places it in front of me.

"Oh my gosh, what is that?" I ask as he dishes up this amazingly aromatic food. He has a small smile on his face.

"This is lemon herb roasted potatoes with seasoned turkey and garlic bread, which is in the shape of a Christmas tree," he announces, and I don't even roll my eyes at the Christmas-themed bread. All I want is to eat it.

He places it down in front of me and it looks heavenly. I don't know if I've even eaten something which looks and smells this amazing.

"All served with mulled wine." He hands me a napkin, and I take it, our hands grazing ever so slightly. Usually, I don't notice it, but today, I do. Even long after his touch disappears, I can still feel the tingle of where it once was.

"Tuck in, I'm curious to hear what you think of my festive dish." Justin takes a bite of his potatoes and he shuts his eyes, savouring the taste.

"Just try it," he encourages me again, and I still hesitate.

"What is this supposed to do?" Surely his big plan isn't to convince me through food. If so, he'll be sorely disappointed.

"Just trust me." is all he says, and I decide I won't argue. I will let him try whatever he wants. Perhaps this is his only form of entertainment, so I will indulge him.

I take a cautionary bite. Immense flavours burst onto my tongue, and I have to hold back a moan. I took a larger piece and savoured the flavours, glad I decided to try it. It's incredible. I won't admit this, but it tastes like Christmas.

"Good?" he asks, grinning like the Cheshire Cat.

"I suppose it's not terrible." Justin laughs heartily and I can't help but join in.

"How about some music?" he asks, already getting up. He grabs his phone from the counter and grins. I know what he is going to do, but it is already in motion.

"You're so transparent. I know exactly what you're..."

"Let It Snow" starts blaring from his phone and I laugh, thinking this perfectly describes the weather right now. Justin sits back down and starts swaying as he eats more potato and turkey.

Once the song is finished, I steal a glance through the window and can't help but worry about how I am going to get home.

"You'll get home, don't worry. The storm won't last all week." His voice is full of the confidence I don't have.

"How do you know? They're saying it's the worst in my lifetime. It's just my luck." I can't stop thinking about the fact I might be stranded with nowhere to go. I play with the strands of my hair as I move the leftover food around my plate, my head leaning on my other hand.

"You won't be stranded, you know. You're more than welcome to stay here if you can't go home." I look up at him, wide eyed. Did I say that out loud, or does he know me that well in such a short time?

"What?"

"Even though you're also very closed off, you're a difficult person to read but, luckily for you, I got an A* in English," he jokes, smirking and raising his eyebrows at me.

"Why doesn't that surprise me?" I say, taking a swig of my wine. As soon as it touches my lips, I have to spit it back into the glass. That is disgusting.

"What the hell is that?" I gag, stuffing some potatoes in my mouth, trying to rid myself of that rancid taste.

"Mulled wine. Don't you like it?" he asks, laughing into his glass.

"No, who would like that? It's disgusting!" I shove some leftover turkey and garlic bread into my mouth, finally ridding myself of that taste. Even though I am certain it will forever be in my nightmares.

"Yeah, I'm not a huge fan of it either, but it's a traditional Christmas drink," he says, getting up and walking towards the fridge.

"But I suppose you're allowed to dislike a few traditional things," he says, throwing me a beer from the fridge, winking. I grin and catch it, not liking how cold the bottle is, but I can deal with that in return for this liquid gold.

"Now you're speaking my language!" I crack it open and take a huge gulp of the beer. It definitely takes my mind off the snow and everything to do with Christmas.

Justin sits back down and opens his beer, leaning back in his chair and giving me an assessing look. It is as if he is evaluating me.

"What?" I question, taking another swig.

"Just thinking about Rose and her getting married." I did not expect that.

"Really, what about it?" I ask. I'm aware that I'm being hypocritical and trying to pry into his life, but I can't help my curiosity.

"I just remember us growing up and she would be in her room with her friends, planning the day she got married. She would make notes, create spread-sheets, and even design picture boards full of ideas." He smiles at the memory and takes another swig. I don't say a word for fear of him not answering.

"Then when she was about fourteen or fifteen, she met a guy who she thought was the love of her life. They did everything together for about a year. She couldn't even brush her hair without him helping." His eyes turn darker.

"He broke up with her for another girl who was going to the same College as him. She was heart-broken and vowed never to date again and certainly never to get married. So she put her books and spreadsheets away. Until she met David." He pauses, leaning forward and placing his hands on the table. "I guess I'm just worried that it will happen again."

"I understand your concern, but she's a big girl and she can handle herself," I say softly so he won't think I'm being patronising. Admittedly, I'm not the best person at giving relationship advice, but I know a thing or two about being independent.

"I know, but when she feels something, she feels it intensely. She loves fearlessly, she hates power-fully, and she cries deeply." I find myself in awe of his words. He is so articulate, and that is something I have rarely found in a man. I have to stop this train of thought before I get off at the wrong station.

"And you'll always be there for her. If she's like me, she'll always find her way. You just need to support her." While I say that, I can't stop thinking about Jasper. He is the only person who fully supports me in every single endeavour. He has since I met him. With every failed relationship and every failed project. He is always there, holding the 'you got this' banner with his shoulder there for me to cry on.

"Have you got anyone who does that for you? You sound like you're speaking from experience," Justin says, taking another swig from his beer.

"Jasper. He's been my rock." Justin's face falls slightly, and if I wasn't watching him, I wouldn't even have noticed. I quickly clear up the fact that Justin is a friend. Nothing more, nothing less.

"He's my best friend from home," I say, not sure why I am even explaining myself.

"Well, he sounds like a great guy." I nod, truly agreeing with him.

"He really is, he's the only person who has stuck by me through everything."

"Even the Christmas thing? Because that's barbaric," Justin jokes, clinking my beer.

"You're not funny," I say, giving him a small smile and taking another drink. I will have to slow down with this drink if I am to commit to my photoshoot to-night.

"Are you ready to get going?" I ask, chugging back the last bit of my beer. He nods, doing the same.

"Shall we clean up?" I pick up my plate and put it by the sink.

"No, I'll do it now. You head up." He takes my place at the sink. Hmm, a man who cleans as well as cooks? I'm impressed.

"Wow, I'm definitely not going to complain. I'm going before you change your mind." I rush out of the door and Justin's laughter rings down the corridor as I run down the hall, trying to remember the way. After lunch, I have a new lease of life. I am walking on clouds and my mood is higher than the tallest mountain on earth.

What makes matters better is that when I walk into the cinema room, it is all done. The lights are put up, and the projector is being set up by David. There is a table in the middle of the room with photos of David and Rose together and a candle. It is perfect, and exactly the type of thing Rose will want. It is almost a perfect copy of what she had shown me in her wedding planner.

"Wow! This is incredible!" I walk around the room and take it all in.

This is everything we need. In fact, we are right on schedule.

"I want it to be perfect for my future wife. I'd do anything for her," David says after he finishes connecting the projector, and it makes me yearn for what they have. I want someone like that for me. Someone who has my back, no matter what. Love is a rare thing. It needs the perfect ingredients to survive. I don't think I'm the right dish for anyone.

"Go get ready, I've got it from here." I push him out of the room. He goes willingly, and I can't stop thinking about what he said. Why can't I find a man like that?

Just as I am finishing up and adding a few tiny details, my phone rings.

It's my Dad.

CHAPTER NINE

I hesitate to answer the phone, but it could be something serious. I shut my eyes tight before answering the phone.

"Hello?"

"Hi, Holly!" It is Sara's cheery voice. She is my father's new wife, and we haven't had the chance to really connect before. Partly because of me, but she irritates me beyond belief.

"Oh, hi, Sara." I don't try to keep the annoyance out of my voice and I don't try to keep the conversation moving forward.

"How have you been?" she asks, the cheeriness fading ever so slightly, but still there.

"What do you want, Sara?" I'm not sure why she always wants to interfere. The older I become, the more her cheeriness makes it harder to see the bad in her.

"I'm just seeing how you are. I'm hoping that we can try to connect a bit," I wander towards the window, trying to give myself strength.

"I'm fine. I'm just really busy with work, that's all." I can hear the laughter of the kids in the background, and I can feel the longing in my stomach. I long for somewhere to call home. I imagine myself there, with my father and Sara, Christmas decorations around us, and the sound of the kids playing rang through the house. But no matter how much I long to feel welcome, something in my mind tells me it is too late. I've shut them out for too long.

"Sara, I've got to go. I'm being called," I say, completely lying as the feeling in my chest tightens.

"Holly?" Sara pauses, her voice quiet. "Just look after yourself, okay?"

"I will." I hang up. My throat closes up, and my head feels fuzzy.

I sit down on the floor, my head in my hands, feeling confused.

"Are you okay?" Justin asks as he walks in.

"Yeah, I'm fine." I get up and start to hang up a few more lights, trying to distract myself from the mess that is my life.

"Are you sure? You don't look fine." He is speaking carefully, as if I am a wild animal who will bolt if he moves too quickly.

I stop and look at him, my eyes heavy, shoulders slumping, and my breath catching.

"Not really."

He sits on the floor and taps the space beside him. I roll my eyes, but don't object.

"I'm all ears," he says, nudging my shoulder. I sit in silence for a few minutes, trying to clear my thoughts. Justin sits there patiently, not pushing me to say something. I respect that more than he would know.

"That was Sara," I say, picking at my finger-nails.

"And she is?" he prompts, gently.

"My stepmother." I pause, and Justin still doesn't push me.

"I wish I could let the past go and be a normal family. I feel like the entire world is crumbling around me, and I don't know how to stop it." I shock myself at the honesty tumbling out of my mouth.

I look at Justin out of the corner of my eye, trying to assess his response. He is still sitting beside me, waiting patiently for me to continue.

"At first, these feelings came from the grief of losing my mother, but now that I'm older it's grown into this horrible bitterness I just can't control."

"You just have to remember who you are. Don't push your family away just because you think they may not understand your emotions. Sometimes, helping them understand is the best way forward. And don't hate Christmas because it brings up a difficult memory. Enjoy it and surround yourself with the family you have because they're the only family you'll ever get," he says. Even though it is hard to hear, I need to hear it.

We sit in silence for a few more minutes, listening to the howling wind outside.

"Grief feels a lot like fear. It's like my own personal prison." I wrap my arms around my legs, hugging them to my chest. Justin gently places his hand on my shoulder.

"Once you let go of that fear, you'll find your freedom. It'll take time, but in the short time I've known you, I know you will manage it. You're stronger than you know. You just have to accept it."

I nod, giving him a genuine smile. "Thanks, Justin."

He says nothing but hands me another beer.

"No, I shouldn't. I have a few more things to finish." I get up and go back to hanging the lights up and try to forget about Sara and the empty seat at their table.

"Come on, it's just one more and it will take the edge off. You need to be cool and collected during the shoot, right?" He knows exactly what he is doing. I sigh, taking another look at him handing me the beer.

"You know, puppy dog eyes don't really work on you." I quickly take the beer and press it up against his neck. He squeals and tries to do the same to me, but I move just in time.

"Ha! You lose," I chant, doing a little happy dance, twirling round and round in circles.

"Not quite." He presses his cold beer against my stomach where my shirt had slightly lifted as I danced. I scream and attempt to get away from the icy touch of beer, but he holds on to me with his other arm.

"I give up!" I yell, laughing and trying to push him off. He is too big for me to budge in any way, so my efforts are totally wasted.

"What? I didn't quite hear you." He presses the bottle against my back and I pound my fist against his arms, laughing and begging to be let go.

"I give up! I'll be nice!" I take one last jab at his arm and he finally lets go of me. It is only then I realised how close we have gotten. His hand is pressed against the small of my back and mine are holding onto his strong, muscular arms. His eyes meet mine, and my heart beats faster. His eyes glance down at my lips, his hands gripping me harder.

"Can anyone help me with this stupid tie?" David asks, waltzing in. Justin and I jump away from each other, blushing. I turn around, facing the wall, trying to catch my breath.

Christ, what the hell is happening?

"Yeah, I'll help," Justin says, clearing his throat. I shut my eyes and smile when I think back to Justin being so close. I can still feel the warmth of his body, and it is like my own personal, exquisite hug.

"Thanks, Justin. Well, I'm all ready. What do you think?" he asks, and I turn just in time to see him spinning round, arms out and showing us his outfit.

He cleans up nicely, wearing a grey suit with his hair slicked back.

"Not too shabby, David," I say, giving him my seal of approval.

"I know, I'm a gorgeous man. You don't have to tell me," he says, fanning himself with a smirk.

"Be careful or your head will get too big for this room!" Justin jokes, throwing him a beer.

"Now all we're waiting for is Rose. I'll go and check on her. Where's her room?" I ask, thinking I'd need a map for this house.

"Upstairs, to the right of the staircase and her room is two doors down from the stairs. If you get lost, her door literally has 'Rose' written in big, bold letters. You can't miss it," David smirks.

As I turn right at the top of the stairs, I chuckle as I see her door instantly. It is bright pink, covered in photos and cheesy pop posters. It also had her name in big, pink letters, just as Justin had said.

Knocking on Rose's door, trying not to ruin her decorations, I kick myself for everything that has happened with Justin so far. I've only just met the man, for God's sake. I am not that desperate.

"Come in!" Rose says from the other side of the door. "Unless you're David, in which case stay out!" I chuckle and open the door a crack.

"It's just me, Grace." Waiting for her to confirm that I can come in. I don't really fancy walking in on anyone getting changed this weekend.

"Grace! Just the person I need to speak to, actually!" She opens the door. She is wearing a silver sequinned dress which fits her figure beautifully. She is wearing an onyx ring, which matches her hair perfectly.

"Rose, you look amazing!" I gush, truly meaning it. I would love to get into a dress like that.

"Really? You think so?" It is the first time since I've met her where I've heard her sound nervous. She usually seems so sure of herself.

"Of course! Wow, these pictures are going to look stunning, we'll make sure of it." She beams a great big smile and claps her hands together.

"I'm so excited." She turns around. "Could you zip me up? I've been trying for the last twenty minutes." I laugh and zip her up, completing the look.

"All done. Are you ready to head up?" I ask, excited to tick one shot off my list. It is always such an amazing feeling for me and the clients. This is the best part.

"I am so ready," she says, grabbing her jacket and following me to the door.

As we walk towards the room, I can't stop myself from saying this.

"You and David are fantastic together."

"Thank you. I truly appreciate it." She grabs my hand and squeezes, giving me a reassuring smile.

"I know you're going to find the same. You just have to open up your heart. When I first met David, I had sworn myself off of all men. I wanted nothing to do with them," she says, still holding my hand.

"I know, Justin briefly mentioned it." I'm not even sure why I say it. Rose gives me a small, sad smile.

"Justin was there for me when no other man was. He's a good guy who has been treated badly by so many people. I would love nothing more than to see him happy." She squeezes my hand tighter.

"But we're not talking doom and gloom now, are we? We have an exciting shoot to do which will be the start of David and I's wedding celebrations." She tears up. "I can't believe I'm getting married soon." She is happy. I can see it. Hell, even a blind person could see it. She's glowing and, again, I want it.

"I'm so happy for you." I truly mean it. She has what everyone dreams of having. A person by your side through thick and thin.

"Thank you, I'm so glad you are the photographer." I can feel tears burning my eyes, which I blink away, and a lump rises in my throat, which I swallow.

Cool, calm and collected, Holly.

"I'm glad too." I can't say anything else because we have arrived at the room. The door is shut, ready for the grand reveal, and Rose squeezes my hand tighter.

"How am I excited but so nervous?" she asks, laughing nervously.

"That's totally normal! But you're going to love it." And I open the door.

Rose gasps and puts her hands over her mouth, eyes wide, as she takes it all in. Justin must have shut the curtains and turned the lights on when I left, which I'm grateful for. In my attempt at getting away from him and the tension between us, I had forgotten the details, which really isn't like me. He has even put on a Christmas movie and set the candles. Usually it'd annoy me if someone took control of my shoot, but today I am thankful. I had gotten distracted when I shouldn't have. That's on me.

"It's amazing!" she says, gasping into her hands and taking it all in.

I look at Justin and nod my thanks. He returns it with a sweet smile. I bite my lip to stop myself from smiling back. This is not the time. I need to be focused now.

"Shall we jump straight in?" I ask, heading to my camera and sorting out the settings. I avoid all eye contact with Justin and focus on getting the perfect shots.

I work for about an hour, taking photos from different angles, until I am happy that we have the perfect pictures. Rose loves the experience and is begging for more when I announce that we are finished.

"Rose, I think Grace has enough photos now. Remember, you'll have other shoots later and she has to edit all of these pictures," Justin says, standing up from his position behind me. He has been a great help with moving props and holding the camera when I had to attend to something in the room, making everything perfect.

Rose pouts. "Plus, you get to watch the film with David now. Think of it as a surprise date. On us." That perks her up.

"Okay! Sounds fun!" She beams, looking at David smiling, excited about watching a Christmas film together. I never understood how watching a film together is a date. You don't talk to each other, so I don't see any point. In fact, I'd only suggest a movie if it was with someone I don't want to talk to.

"Shall we?" Justin asks, holding out his arm.

"Have fun, guys!" I say, and dump the equipment in Justins arms outstretched arm, flashing him a grin as I walk out in the hall.

"I should probably start editing the photos." He nods, "I'll see you tonight?" I ask, taking the equipment from his arms.

"I'll see you tonight," he says, chuckling to himself. His smile and laugh is contagious, and I know I'm in trouble.

I shake away that feeling and walk back to my room. I can feel his eyes follow me down the hallway, but I don't turn around.

It is almost two hours later by the time I finish editing the last photo, and my eyes feel so sore from looking at a screen for so long. Besides the eye pain and the headache, I am happy. The photos have turned out perfectly, and I can't wait to show them to Rose and David. In fact, I want to show the whole damn household.

Getting up, I stretch my legs and hear a knock on the door. I dash over to the door, excited to show someone these photos.

It's always an exceptional moment when you have a successful photoshoot. Not all of them lead to great photos, and I know about that all too well. Especially when I was first starting out.

I fling back the door, my smile disappearing when I see that it's Justin.

"Wow, you look incredibly unhappy to see me."

I scoff. "You just weren't who I was expecting, that's all. I thought it might have been Rose coming by to have a look at the photos." He crosses his arms and leans against the doorframe, not saying a word.

"What do you want, Justin?"

"Aren't you going to let me in?" Sighing, I step aside, at least I will be able to show someone the photos, even if it wasn't Rose. He steps in and closes the door.

"How are the photos?" he asks.

"Glad you asked." I pick up the laptop and hand it to him, letting him flick through the pictures.

He is looking at them for a while in silence while I am waiting and watching, biting my fingernails.

"These are amazing," he finally says, putting the laptop down and looking at me with admiration. Under his gaze, I felt like the most talented woman.

"Thank you," I whisper. I can feel those butterflies creeping back up. Maybe I shouldn't have invited him in.

"Was there something you wanted?" I ask, staying as far away from him as I can.

"I heard some of your conversation with your step mother, and I wanted to cheer you up. Put on your shoes," he instructs, getting up from my bed and walking to the door. I laugh scornfully, and he turns, giving me a questioning look.

"So Justin Williams comes to my room and I'm supposed to be ready to go whenever you summon me?" I ask, not quite believing what he was saying.

"Women always manage to make things sound so dramatic." He grins and opens the door. "Just come on." He disappears out of the room. My curiosity is going to get me into some trouble one day.

I, of course, follow. I suppose it can't hurt as I'd completed my jobs for the day, so I'm facing a few hours of boredom before dinner.

"Is this something to do with the bet?" I ask, already suspecting this to be the case. I've noticed in the short time I've been here that he is just as competitive as I am.

"Of course it is. I think you're going to say you hate it but secretly love it," he responds, and I'm scared. This bet is only fun and games, but there is also an ugly truth; I fear Justin will think I'm bitter and mean if he digs into the real reason I dislike Christmas.

"Will you just give me a hint?" I ask, dragging my fingers against the tinsel running along the banister. It looks so tacky, but I'm starting to doubt whether I truly think that or if it is just a habit I have developed.

"You're really impatient." He pauses. "I think I've said that before." I roll my eyes.

"Yeah, and you're slightly full of yourself." I say, chucking him a smile so he knows I'm joking. Justin chuckles.

"That's your opinion." He turns to me and winks. He finally stops at a door, but this one is different. This one has no decorations at all which, for this house, is strange. Really strange.

"What's in there?" I ask, staring at this blank, undecorated door.

"Why do you sound so scared?"

"You've taken me to the only door with no decorations. Knowing your family, they wouldn't just leave it undecorated. What's in there? The real life Grinch? A poltergeist? A kidnapper?" Justin lets out a booming laugh, smacking the wall as he wipes the tears from his eyes. I just stand there, arms folded and wait for him to finish.

Once he has wiped the tears from his eyes, and quietened down to a chuckle, I point towards the door.

"Now what's in there?" I don't take a single step towards it.

"Have a look." He opens the door and, as it slowly creaks open. I brave a peek. I reach out to grab Justin's arm, just in case something jumps out. He softly laughs at me, but I ignore him.

One eye can now see into the room and I can't see anything. It is just a normal room. I become braver and poke my head further in, confused by why he brought me here.

"What is this room?" I walk inside and can see a small fireplace in the middle of the room, a coffee table, a cream sofa, and a large TV. There isn't much else besides a few boxes in one corner of the room.

"It's my old playroom. I used to hang out here all the time as a kid with my sister." He walks into the room and lays his hand on the back of the sofa, clearly reminiscing about the memories this room holds.

"I thought playrooms were supposed to be colourful and full of toys?" I ask, noticing the bland white and cream colouring.

"When we both went off to College, my parents repainted the room and there was a plan to turn this into a reading room. They never really finished, so it's kind of been left like this." So it's abandoned.

"So, what are we doing here?" I ask again, truly not understanding what he is trying to do. He gives me a sheepish grin and walks towards the boxes in the room's corner.

"Please, no more storage. I'm fed up with storage." I moan, not able to think of anything worse than sorting out another room. That will do the opposite of what he said he would do. I will finally hate Christmas.

"It's not storage. It's something a lot more fun." He pulls back the lid of the box and he is wrong. It is worse than storage.

"Oh no, no, no. No way." I back away, trying to leave the room. He rushes towards me, gently pulling on my arm, bringing me back into the room.

"Oh, come on, I think you'll enjoy it!" he says, pouting and giving me his poor attempt at puppy dog eyes.

"Again, those don't work for you." He rolls his eyes.

"Come on, you said you would take the bet, so that means doing everything I say."

He is right. Crap.

"Fine, but don't think for one second that I'll enjoy it." I say, crossing my arms. He bites his lip, trying to hide the smile that is threatening to form. It is too late. I've already seen it and I am annoyed that he is so confident.

"Let's get this over with." I storm up to the boxes and look inside. They are full of Christmas decorations, from a small tree to wads of tinsel. Even a sprig of mistletoe.

"You've got to be joking," I whisper, really regretting taking that deal.

"My parents never got round to decorating this room, so I thought it was perfect for you to do it. Find the pleasure of Christmas by decorating a room," he says, holding his hands out. I put my hands on my hips, not looking impressed.

"Let's get started then. I'm getting hungry," I say, trying to speed this up.

I take out the tree, which is in several pieces, already hating this.

"Not a fresh tree like every other tree in your house?" I ask. "Run out of your tree money fund and have to slum it with a plastic tree?"

"No, this room isn't really used, so we settled for a plastic one." He watches me struggle to know which part went where. "Have you ever even put up a tree?"

"No, I haven't. I've helped my mother decorate the tree, but I've never put a whole tree up myself." I confess.

"Okay, well we're going to change that." He is sincere, which makes me feel even worse. "Let me help you."

"Every year my family would decorate the tree together. It's become a tradition." I wonder what having a family tradition would be like. I don't have any.

We start assembling the tree, piece by agonising piece. Halfway through, Justin goes to 'fetch' something and comes back with his phone speakers. No matter how hard I object, he still blasts Christmas music.

"You know you could actually listen to normal music?" I say after the fifth repetition of "Baby, it's cold outside."

"You know you could try to be a little less negative," he says, tossing a bauble at me. I catch it, giving him a victorious smile as I add it to the tree. I hold up the string of lights that Justin passed to me from the box, and place them on the tree, realising we should have done this first and the baubles after.

"I think we've done it wrong," I say, laughing as the baubles start falling off and the lights become tangled.

"I'm sure this is how my mother does it," he says, trying to catch the baubles.

"I don't think so, Justin. Maybe we need to start again." He nods, letting the baubles fall to the floor. It takes another thirty minutes before the lights and baubles are taken down and we re-wrap the tree with the lights and hang up the baubles. The branches of the tree are now holding them in place, and they show no signs of the struggles Justin and I had just dealt with.

We both stand back, observing the tree, and I feel an immense sense of pride. This is the first tree I have decorated or even put up since my mother died. I forgot the feeling of accomplishment that it creates, and my eyes tear up. It's a tall, bright, glossy green tree, with a shining gold star at the top. The tinsel and lights are wrapped all the way around the tree, with ornaments hanging from each branch.

"It's beautiful." I sniffle.

"There's more," Justin promises, plugging the lights into the socket. I'm not sure I am prepared for this, but I have no time to be. Justin flips the switch and the tree bursts into a dozen colours. There are bright, twinkling lights in the shades of yellow, red, blue, gold, and purple.

I am impressed by how magical and beautiful it looks, and the feeling I feel standing there gazing upon this tree stirs up memories.

I can remember standing next to my parents, gazing up at the tallest tree I had ever seen. We covered it in red ribbons and baubles containing our pictures and I could remember feeling the excitement of Christmas. I could feel my mother's hand gently hold on to my shoulder, pulling me closer to her as she and my father gazed into each other's eyes, totally in love. I remember wondering if I would ever find that.

"Grace? Are you okay?" I hear Justin ask, and all I can do is nod. I don't trust my voice as the feelings slowly fade away and I am back in the current moment.

After a few more seconds, I can breathe again. "I'm fine, I just haven't decorated a tree since…" I pause. Justin knows what I am going to say and touches my shoulder gently, just as my mother once did.

CHAPTER TEN

The bet is well under way.

After we have decorated the room upstairs, Justin had me make my very own Christmas card at the kitchen table with his entire family while we tuck in to some freshly baked cookies. I take photos of everyone together as they want to record as many moments together as possible. Truthfully, I thought this would be agony, but I feel welcome and I see how well they connect as a family, and I want it. I was feeling things I haven't felt in nearly nine years.

Afterwards, Justin and I make some hot chocolate and sit in the conservatory, watching the snow drift down. The clock gently chimed seven in the background as we gazed out at the night sky. It's silent outside, as I can't hear the dogs barking or the owls hoot. Everything and everyone is settling down for the night. It is peaceful, not like back home in Cardiff where cars honk their horns, and sirens are blaring down the street. I sit there, watching as the snow continues to fall, slowly adding to the gradually melting layers already on the floor.

"Do you think it'll stop soon?" I ask, blowing on my hot chocolate.

"I don't know. I hope so." I have a sudden spike of anxiety, thinking that he wants to get rid of me as soon as possible.

"Maybe phone your dad? The news said they've cancelled travel for at least another few days."

"Yeah, okay. I'll see what he thinks I should do. Maybe he will come and get me?" I suggest, making the plans in my head.

"No, I don't think any travel is a good idea. I've said before, you're more than welcome to stay here for as long as you need."

"You just want more days to win the bet," I joke, bumping my arm against his. He chuckles, taking a swig from his hot chocolate.

"How am I doing?" he asks, his voice deeper and softer as he leans closer to me. I can feel my heart thundering under my shirt, scared he might see it. I gulp and drink some more hot chocolate, giving myself some precious seconds to think about my reply.

"I still can't stand Christmas music, but give it a few days and I'll let you know." I don't know how I feel about any of it yet. I can't deny the fact I am feeling differently about a few things.

"I'll ring my dad," I say, desperately wanting a subject change.

"Okay, want me to leave you to it?" he asks, about to place his hot chocolate down. I shake my head, tapping the space next to me so he stays with me.

I pull out my phone and dial my dad's number, hoping he won't bring up Sara's phone call. Knowing him, that'll be the first thing he brings up.

"Holly?" He sounds as if he had been running again.

"Hi, Dad, did I interrupt something"

"No, no. You are welcome to call anytime. Night or day. How are you?" he asks, clearing his throat.

"I'm good, I'm just calling to ask your advice, actually."

"Anything." His breathing has settled and I can hear his happiness that I've called, and I actually miss him. I've missed hearing his voice sound so upbeat.

"I'm still in England, and the storm shows no signs of slowing down. Do you think I should try getting home now or wait it out?" I ask, biting my fingernails. Deep down, I already know the answer I want him to give.

"Cardiff is snowed-in. All travel is cancelled and I won't be able to pick you up, Holly," he says, and I can hear the disappointment in his voice. I know he wants to help me out, but he can't.

"No, no, it's fine! Justin said I could stay with them for however long I need," I say, looking at Justin to confirm this is, in fact, still the case. He nods, flashing me a small smile. My heart flutters.

"Are they nice? Treating you well?"

"Yeah, they're extremely nice. Christmas fanatics, but nice." Justin scoffs, but doesn't seem surprised I said it. I flash him a wink, which he ignores.

"I bet you're loving that," my father says, chuckling. I am about to update him on everything that has happened this week, but I can hear one of the kids and Sara in the background.

"Holly, I'm sorry, but I'm going to have to shoot off. They're trying to go out to play in the snow again and will probably catch hypothermia if I don't put a stop to this," he says, already sounding like he is rushing down the hall.

A small part of me feels sad, but I don't let it show on my face. Not with Justin sitting next to me, watching my face.

"Okay. Uh, yeah that's totally fine." We both go quiet for a second, trying to think of the next thing to say.

"Just keep me updated, Holly." He sounds worried, and I want him to know I am okay.

"I will, but I'm truly okay."

We talk for a few more minutes before I hang up the phone and drink some more hot chocolate, trying to avoid the inevitable questions from Justin. It doesn't work for long.

"What happened?" he asks, inching closer.

I sigh. "He just had to shoot off to the boys."

I watch the snow falling and feel my dislike of it slowly lessening. I can acknowledge now that there is a certain beauty to the snowflakes gently floating down. Maybe that is because I'm not in it, freezing cold, losing all feeling in my limbs. Or is it because this is the first Christmas since my mother died that I don't feel alone? I feel welcomed for the first time and I like it. I don't want anything to ruin this feeling.

"What are you thinking about?" he asks, gazing off into the snow.

"What it would be like to go ice skating." I don't know where this came from. I have never thought of that before, so why now?

"Have you ever been?" he asks.

"No. My mother booked for us to go skating in Cardiff, but she died before we could go. It was going to be my first time."

"You say those kinds of things with no emotion. Like you're numb to it." I look at him and see a deep sadness in his eyes. I feel uncomfortable at the thought that he feels sorry for me.

"If I'm emotional every time I think or talk about her, I wouldn't get anything done." I try to joke, but it falls flat and Justin just looks at me knowingly.

"Don't," he says. "Don't do that."

I scoff. "Do what?"

"Don't deflect from something which upsets you. It's perfectly okay to not be okay." I have heard of that saying before, but I have never truly understood it until this moment. I clear my throat knowing if I don't change the subject, I will become a crying mess, and I don't want to ruin the moment.

"Have you ever ice skated?" I ask, taking a long swig of my hot chocolate, glad it has cooled to a manageable temperature, trying to steady my breathing and blink away the tears which threaten to fall.

"Yeah, I have. There's a lake near the house which I skate on when it's frozen over." He points at the trees in the garden. "Just behind those trees there."

"I wish I could go skating." We both fall into a comfortable silence for a few minutes, watching as the snow continues to gather outside. It is magical, and I feel the sudden urge to go out in it. I want to dance in the snow and make snowmen and snow angels and go ice-skating. I swallow that feeling down, knowing I have to go and get some sleep.

"I'd better get going," I say, getting up and grabbing my now empty hot chocolate mug from the floor. He also gets up, stretching his legs and yawning.

"Yeah, me too. Who knows what tomorrow may bring?" he suggests.

I wonder the same thing.

CHAPTER ELEVEN

"Grace, wake up!" Rose is knocking on the door very loudly. I groan, hiding my head under the duvet, trying to drown out the sounds of her fists beating on the wood.

"I'll be out in a second!" I grumble, wanting to turn over and sleep for another few hours.

"Are you decent? Can I come in?" She asks, still tapping on the blasted door. I pull the duvet closer to my face, but the knocking still manages to infiltrate my ears.

"I'm in bed, but go for it." I'm glad I don't have to get up and open the door myself. Pulling back the duvet, I rub my eyes trying to wake myself up. Whatever Rose wants, I know it will take too much energy for this time in the morning.

She skips in and opens up the curtains. Sunshine streams into the room almost blinding me. I squeal and hide my face in my pillows.

"Is this the thanks I get for taking amazing photos of you?" I ask, "Being woken up and blinded at, what I assume to be, five in the morning?" She laughs lightly and I want to throw my pillows at her.

"It's ten, actually." She tries tugging at the duvet, but I'm a fighter and I won't let it go.

"Feels like it's five." I pull back the duvet, exposing myself to the freezing cold air. Goosebumps form on my skin and I grab my trusted, cosy dressing gown. I groan, not even wanting to look at my reflection in the mirror. From the corner of my eye, I can see that my hair is sticking out in several directions and my face is incredibly pale. For that, I blame living in the UK. You can never get a decent tan because of the unpredictable weather.

"Well, you're definitely going to love what we've got planned for you." She gives me a knowing smile. Someone in the corridor clears their throat, and she rolls her eyes.

"What *Justin* has planned."

"I have absolutely no idea what you're talking about, Rose."

"Just get changed and meet us downstairs in fifteen minutes!" She picks up my jumper and leaves it on the chair beside the door.

"Make sure you dress warm." She winks and leaves, closing the door behind her.

This family is awfully strange, but in the few days I've known them, I've grown to enjoy their eccentricity. There is always something going on and they are very entertaining.

I have my non-negotiable warm shower and throw on my super warm jeans and the jumper that Rose had laid out for me. It isn't a Christmas jumper so I'm grateful for small mercies. Who knows what kind of monstrosity this Christmas-loving family would force me into given half the chance.

I'm five minutes late, but I needed that shower. I won't do anything productive until I feel refreshed and awake.

Walking into the kitchen, everyone is eating their breakfast and whispering about something. As soon as I walk into the room, the conversation stops and I know they have been talking about me.

"What are you guys talking about?"

"Your surprise." Rose says, grinning like the Cheshire Cat. Justin kicks her from under the table and she shoots him the dirtiest look I've ever seen from her.

"What surprise?" I ask, getting excited. If I am being honest, I am loving this bet, but I certainly won't admit that to Justin.

"Come and see," he says, getting up from the table and grabbing his coat. He hands me some toast, helps me put my coat on, and I feel like I could float on air. I become suspicious of this feeling, and I automatically go on alert. I always do this. I start becoming close with someone and my mind will scream at me that I will lose them. 'Don't get too close.' And I never do.

His entire family follows suit, putting their coats on as well. His grandparents are still sitting in their chairs, smiling and waving us off.

"Your grandparents aren't coming?" I ask.

"No, she can't go sadly, but she can see where we're going from the window upstairs. Arthur will stay with her and make sure she's alright." That makes sense, but it didn't stop me feeling guilty that she couldn't come.

"I'll grab my camera. We need more outdoor pictures," I say, not forgetting that I'm here to work.

Before we leave the house, Justin's dad picks up a large bag. I don't have time to ask what is in it as everybody heads outside. People are shouting questions, asking if everyone is ready and has everything they need. The snow is still coming down, but the wind has eased slightly. It's still enough to dishevel my hair, but it's bearable. As we step outside, I can feel the crunch of freshly fallen snow beneath my boots and I relish in the feeling, actually enjoying it for once. Before this job, I would have shuddered and wished to be back on freshly cut grass, but now, I'm appreciating it more.

I am still absolutely freezing, but I feel free for the first time in a long time.

We chat quietly as a group while Justin and Rose lead us towards our snowy destination. We have been walking for a few minutes when we come to a clearing.

In front of us is a beautiful frozen lake.

"Oh my gosh, is that the lake?" I ask, looking at the glistening snow on the surrounding trees and bushes and the ice which has covered the surface of the lake. It is utterly gorgeous, and it takes my breath away. Justin turns back to me, his eyes twinkling with excitement.

"It is. I thought you could try ice skating for the first time here," he says, scratching his neck. He looks worried.

I love it. It is the sweetest thing that anyone has done for me in a long time, and I am full of gratitude and joy. I can feel the happiness bubbling out of me and I am itching to get out on the ice. I take a few steps towards Justin, nervousness creeping through my body.

"I want to, but I'm nervous. When I've seen people do this in the past, it has looked quite dangerous." Glancing at the ice, I want to run towards it, but I also want to get far, far away from it.

"You have me. I'll go around with you and I won't let you fall, okay?" he says softly. Biting my lip, I nod. Once it is confirmed that I am skating, Rose rushes towards me with the giant bagGeorge had been carrying and pulls out some ice skates. Ah, so that was what was in the bag.

"You look like you have the same shoe size as me, so try them on!" she squeals, practically shoving them in my face. I laugh, swapping my camera bag for the skates in her hand.

I pull them on, overjoyed that they fit, and it almost feels like a Cinderella moment.

I stand up, Rose and Justin gently holding onto my arms.

"This feels unnatural..." I say, trying to keep my balance. A big gust of wind almost topples me, but I keep my balance.

"You're doing great." Evelyn's voice is calming, mixed in with the chaos of the wind, and it gives me confidence. I ignore the snow swirling in my face and the wind threatening to knock me down, and I slowly make my way towards the ice.

Justin and Rose take it in turns to hold me up, while the other puts on their skating boots. Once they're done, we inch towards the ice. I am still safely on the ground, ready to embark on an icy adventure. As I carefully step onto the makeshift rink, I can hear my mother's reassuring words. *'Holly, I believe in you. I will always be with you.'* That gives me an immense amount of confidence.

I can feel my body tingling with excitement while my muscles are tensing and shaking as the nerves and the excitement mix into one.

"You're doing amazing!" Rose shouts, spitting the snow out of her mouth. I laugh, but the vibrations caused by my laughter make me shake and I almost fall back. Justin catches my arms, and I laugh even harder. I am having such an amazing time, I don't want to leave.

I cling onto Justin, like a small child would cling to their mother.

He slowly skates backwards, taking me with him. My legs don't dare move.

"Oh my gosh, I'm kinda doing it!" I shout, shocked that I am actually standing on ice. It is a crazy concept to me, but I am doing it.

A flash comes from behind me, and I try to turn to see where it is coming from. Justin pulls me back.

"It's okay, it's just my mother taking a photo. Just keep focusing on me." He is so calm and collected, which makes me feel fearless. It is a different feeling from anything I have ever experienced before. This is thrilling, even though I am absolutely terrified. It is like I am flying in a plane for the first time, or learning to swim or ride a bike. They all feel so different, but exciting. My blood is pumping and all I want to do is run, scream, and whoop in the air.

Justin goes a little faster, skating like a professional. I still don't move my legs, in fear of taking us both down and falling flat on my arse. I just allow myself to glide after Justin, getting used to this alien feeling.

"You okay?" he asks, flicking his head to re-move the hair from his eyes. He still hasn't let go of me, and for that I am grateful.

"Look, I'm amazing!" I yell, laughing and almost falling back again. I don't fall because Justin has a firm hold of me. He grins, looking at me differently to how he's ever looked at me before. He looks mesmerised and I can't help but stare back. His hair is slightly damp from the snow, with some flakes still stuck in his hair. His face is slightly red from the cold, and I could've stared at him for hours.

Another flash appears behind me, breaking us out of the trance. This time, I turn around and am shocked to see we are what looks like miles away from everyone else.

"Oh my gosh, is that how far we've skated?" I cry, letting the nerves creep back in. If anything were to happen, we would be screwed. If I fall in the lake, I'll die before anyone can get to us.

Justin sees my fear and gently shakes me, so that I am looking at him again.

"You're fine. I've got you, and I won't let you go." He says it so sternly, I nod believing him instantly. I know he has me.

Rose comes barrelling past us with David, hand in hand. They are laughing and teasing each other about how fast they could go, making it a race. I wish I could do it. I want to stop relying on Justin and gain some of my independence back.

"Let go and I'll see if I can do it by myself," I say, fully confident in myself.

"Are you sure?"

"Yeah." He lets go of me one hand at a time until I am standing by myself. Justin doesn't go far. In fact, he is still holding his hands out in case I fall.

Slowly, I move my feet, tripping occasionally but never falling. The longer I skate by myself, the more my smile grows and the more confident I feel.

I laugh, barely moving one mile an hour. He laughs and claps, encouraging me to keep going. I'm not the most graceful skater, but I am doing it, and I am so happy. I feel free.

The snow has picked up, so everyone starts to head back to the house. As I walk back, it shocks me to realise how different skating feels to walking. In fact, the entire walk back I am bouncing and skipping, laughing with Rose about how my legs now felt like jelly.

"I took loads of pictures on your camera. I have to say, it's fantastic quality! Made me feel like a real professional," Evelyn says, handing me back my camera once we are inside.

"It was a gift from my best friend, actually. It's a great camera and I honestly don't know what I would do without it," I say, placing it back into its bag.

"Well, who wants some hot chocolate?" she asks, already heading into the kitchen. Marilyn and Arthur have made their way back downstairs, congratulating me on how well I skated.

"Maybe we can start on the charity bags?" Rose asks, following Evelyn into the kitchen.

"Charity bags?" I ask.

"Yeah, we do them every year. We collect essentials and some gifts and treats and put them in bags for the homeless or those who don't have as much as we do," Rose explains, and everyone follows her into the kitchen. I didn't even know that is something people did at Christmas. Does that make me a bad person?

Evelyn goes into the pantry and instructs George to grab the heavy shopping bags while Justin turns on the hob for another batch of hot chocolate. I can feel my limbs defrosting, and I can finally feel my nose again.

I am still on a high from ice skating, and I just want to go back out and do it again. I am definitely going to go with Jasper when I get home, and the thought of his surprise makes me smile.

"What are you smiling about?" Marilyn asks, giving me a knowing smile. "Or should I say, who is making you smile?" Why would she assume I'm smiling because of someone? I ask myself. I instantly look at Justin as he pauses at the stove and tilts his head towards us.

"Just thinking about how I can't wait to show Jasper that I can skate." I chuckle.

"Oh, is Jasper your fella?" she asks, and I'm not sure if she remembered our conversation from the first day we met. When she wondered why a girl like me could ever be single. Something in me wanted to say, *'yes, Jasper is my man.'* But I can't. My eyes flicker to Justin's tense back, and then back to his grandmother's waiting eyes.

"No, he's my best friend," I answer, and I can see Justin go back to making the hot chocolate, which makes me wonder. She nods, and doesn't push me any further, for which I am very grateful for.

"Have you ever done these before, Grace?" Evelyn tips the bag's contents onto the empty table. There are toothbrushes and toothpaste, sanitary products, socks, snacks, dry food, hand sanitiser, and so much more.

"No, I haven't. Do you really do this every year?" I ask, wondering why I've done nothing like this. I don't have to like Christmas to help people.

"Yep, every year without fail."

I have gained a whole new level of respect for this family.

They place all the items on the table while Justin places the hot chocolates in front of us. I waste no time in taking a swig, burning my lips, but I don't care.

Rose puts some Christmas music on and they show me how to prepare the Christmas bags. It's easy. You just take one thing from each pile and place them in the bag and seal it up, putting it in a box on the floor.

We sit there for at least thirty minutes packing bags, singing and dancing, and I join in, dancing in circles.

"We need to photograph this moment!" Marilyn yells over the music, clapping. I don't have to be asked twice, and I fetch my camera, which is on the shelf by the front door.

"Do you want casual photos or do you want more formal poses?" I ask, setting up the camera.

"I think a bit of both, dear."

"No problem, let's do the candids first."

I walk around the table, taking photos of everyone dancing and putting items in the bags. After I take the candid ones, I get everyone to stand up by the table, and take a few group ones. Once we are done, I am about to put the camera back, but Rose and David start dancing to "Last Christmas" and the artist in me wants to capture this moment.

I am so happy with the photos I have taken, and I feel at peace. The only thing that I can't think about is my father. I'm not ready for that yet.

Just thinking about him brings all of the guilt and sadness back, and looking at this family dancing and singing and laughing, I know I will be facing a silent apartment when I get home.

"I think I have all the pictures I need." I put my camera away. "I might go and edit them, actually. See you later," I say, wanting to leave this room now.

"Are you okay?" Rose asks. I nod, but say nothing. I remember that once the blizzard eases up, I'll be heading home soon and I will see my father. This saddens me. Not because I want to stay, but because I want what they have.

No one objects to me leaving, and for that, I'm thankful. I go up to my room and shut the door, trying my hardest not to cry.

How can my mood change so fast? I was elated after skating. I hadn't felt that happy in what feels like forever. So what changed that?

I already know the answer. It's my dad. I can't stop thinking about him. Here I am, having the best Christmas I've had since my mom died, and it's with another family.

There is a knock at the door and I wipe the few tears which got past my defences and open the door.

It is, of course, Justin.

"Yes?" I ask with a slight edge to my voice.

"Come with me," he says. I try to shut the door. I'm not in the mood for another part of his bet. In fact, I want a nap and to wallow in self-pity for a while.

"Come on. I think this will cheer you up." His smile reaches his eyes and I can't say no. I guess it will be nice to have some company.

I point my finger. "Fine, but I'm seriously not happy about it."

"You don't have to be. Just comply and follow me."

"I'll comply with a fist in your mouth if you carry on." I joke and he laughs. I chuckle, already enjoying his company. He is very similar to Jasper because he doesn't take my crap. In fact, they both give as good as they get.

He is taking me towards the room we had turned into a cinema, and my suspicions are correct when he stopped at that very door.

"I have the perfect Christmas film choices for you," he says, wagging his eyebrows and inviting me in. I reluctantly walk in, hoping it isn't the typical 'Home Alone' film.

I haven't watched a Christmas film in years, so he had a job cut out for him... again.

I sit down and wrap a fluffy blanket around me, letting him do all the dirty work. He made me come up here so I will not touch a damn thing.

"What are your choices, then?" I am very apprehensive. I'm scared to have hope for this film, because if I don't enjoy it, then all the positivity I've gained so far will be ruined. I will feel like I am taking steps back, not forward. In fact, I wish I was back in my room, sleeping. I should've listened to myself, but I got distracted by him and his damned smile.

""The Grinch" or "A Christmas Carol"?" he asks, shooting me a sly smile. Usually I'd find that funny, but at the moment, I'm not feeling quite myself.

"Okay, I'll see you later." I get up from the beanbag, not wanting to deal with this. I don't have the energy today.

"Grace, what's wrong?" Justin asks, stopping me from leaving the room.

"Absolutely everything is wrong," I cry, quickly turning to face him. He frowns, clearly not knowing what to say.

"Grace, please talk to me. You were so happy earlier, out on the lake."

"That wasn't real, not really. That was a fantasy because that wasn't my life."

"How? It can be if you let it," he says, like it is so simple. Like I can go home and live a happy life without my mother.

"You don't know me, so you can't possibly understand." Tears have fallen down my cheeks, which makes me even angrier. I don't want to cry. In fact, I'm annoyed that I've allowed my professionalism to leave me. I wouldn't be like this with any other client. So why him?

"I know you miss your mum. I know you're hurting, I understand," he says, trying to keep his voice neutral, but I can still hear the slight tremor.

"You don't understand! How could you possibly understand? You have your family and your stupidly big house." His nose flares, and I know I hit a nerve.

"Don't. Just because you're upset doesn't mean you can take it out on me, okay?"

I say nothing, unsure of how I can fix this now. I know I don't want to hurt Justin, but I can't stop the words from spilling out of my mouth.

Justin sighs, placing his hands on his hips. "Talk to me. What's going on in your head?" His face is no longer red and angry, but scared and worried. He frowns, his shoulders relaxing and his fists unclenching.

My shoulders sag. "Everything hurts for me, Justin. I go home to an empty apartment, my family is practically non-existent, and don't forget about my mother," I angrily wipe my tears away. I'm not angry at Justin, I'm angry at how I have allowed my life to turn into this mess. How did it get so bad?

"What do you mean? You've never spoken about your family." I can tell he's pushing, so I will give him what he wants. In my usual fashion, I will push him away, just like I do to every other guy. I don't know why he is any different, or why I am trying to protect him.

"When I was younger, my father found Sara so quickly after my mother's death. I felt like my mother and I meant nothing to him." I cry.

"Grace, please understand your father de-served to move on. It doesn't mean he doesn't love you." I know he would say that. And I know he is right. I think I've known for a while, but the bitterness inside of me was too thick to cut through.

"I know that now. But it's too late for my family and I. You don't understand." It is as if he has flicked a switch and all the anger and frustration comes rushing back into his eyes. His jaw clenches and his back tenses.

"Stop saying that. I understand. I'm trying to help you, Grace."

"My name isn't Grace. It's Holly," I spit, the words tasting like poison. His face falls, and he staggers back slightly.

"Now do you understand the person I am? I don't even like the name my mother gave me."

"So you decided to lie to me? To my family?" I instantly regret lying about my name and I want to fix my mistake. I want to fix myself, to change who I am. I don't want to be the girl who hurts people because she is hurting. But I am.

I walk towards him, my hand outstretched. He grabs it and brings it to his lips. I sob and grasp his hand tighter, wanting to apologise. But someone bursts into the room, and we break apart. I hadn't noticed how close we were until the spell was broken.

It is his grandmother and Rose. They both look back and forth between us, clearly noticing the tension which must have permeated the room. I wipe the tears from my burning cheeks.

"You guys okay?" Rose asks.

"Yeah, we're fine. What's up?" he asks, clearing his throat and running his fingers through his hair.

"I just want to tell you that travel has opened back up. You can go home," Rose says, her eyes stare into Justin's, asking if he is okay with her eyes. Marilyn's eyes are flickering between Justin and I.

Upon hearing that travel has reopened, my heart sinks. I want to fix things with Justin, but I know I'm not good for him. I break everything I touch.

"That's just perfect." I shoot a fake smile, wasting no time in charging out of the room and running up to my room. I can hear everyone calling after me, but I don't turn around.

CHAPTER TWELVE

I waste no time in calling for a taxi. I pull out my suit-case and pack my bags, tears streaming down my face. It's like someone cursed me to ruin every good thing in my life. I've messed up the chance of having this family as an ongoing client, as well as a friendship with them. Maybe I'm not destined to have friends or people close to me. I have been lonely from the moment my mother died. I don't know why I thought that could change.

There's a knock on my door, and I want to scream. I want to be left alone, as I should be. I say nothing, nor do I open the door. I want to finish packing my things and leave. The sooner I go, the less damage I'll do.

The door opens, and I'm expecting Justin, but it isn't. It's Marilyn.

"Grace- uh, I mean Holly?" she says, shuffling slowly into the room. I immediately rush over to help, gently taking her arms and leading her to the bed. I tell myself to be patient because I'm not angry with her, but I'm vibrating with the urge to get out of here.

"Justin has told me some things," she says. I slowly lower her to the bed, helping her sit down. She gently taps the space next to her, inviting me to sit. I don't.

She sighs. "Okay, do what makes you feel comfortable. All I ask is that you let me speak," she carefully chooses her words. I nod, not believing that what she is going to say will change my mind.

"I am terribly sorry to hear about your mother. But you mustn't blame your father." Great, another person to tell me what I should feel.

"If you're going to sit there and tell me I'm wrong, then you can leave. I have packing to do." I hate this side of me, but I know once it comes out, it is very hard to put my attitude back in the box.

"Darling, come and sit. I have a brief story for you, and I think it will help." She doesn't seem phased at all by my outburst. I bite my lip, trying to suppress the bitterness within me. I guess the rational Holly would sit down and let her talk. She's ill, after all.

I take a breath and finally sit next to her. She cradles my hands.

"I was engaged to be married to my first boy-friend. I loved him dearly, and in some ways, I still do."

"What happened? Is that Arthur?" I ask, and she shakes her head.

"No, he died." My heart aches for her. I clutch her hand tighter as the anger in me evaporates.

"I'm so sorry." She tightens her hands on mine, telling me it's okay, and carries on.

"We met when we were young, and a few years later, they drafted him to go into the army. We, of course, kept in touch through letters and I remember be-ing so excited the day the mail-carrier came and did his rounds." She pauses, smiling at the memory.

"In the letters, he promised he would propose to me the day we saw each other again, when he was back safe from the war. He kept that promise, and the day he came back, we were engaged." She sounds younger as she retells the story.

"We were so happy. I remember the feeling like it was yesterday. But, we weren't meant to be." She pauses again, bracing herself for the next part. "He died a few weeks before the wedding. A hit and run." I gasp, tears threatening to fall from my eyes.

"That's awful!" My voice cracks as I think about how hard it must've been for her.

"How did you cope?" I ask, needing her an-swer. I know I'm not coping.

She smiles and wipes away my tears. Her eyes are dry and full of happiness. How did she do it?

"I met my Arthur when I was so lonely and in the middle of my grief. I tried to push him away. I cannot count how many times I tried, but he stuck with me like glue. It took me years to open up to him and even longer to realise we were in love." She looks me straight in the eye. "Holly, I waited too long to be happy, and all I was really doing was torturing myself. The day I let Arthur in, and I accepted everything, was the day I found happiness again. True happiness. Don't wait so long like I did," she insists, her eyes begging me to listen to her.

My phone rings.

"It's the taxi to pick me up," I say, scratching my neck, feeling conflicted. She lets go of my hands and smiles at me kindly.

"Sometimes everything you need is right under your nose. I know you'll choose the right thing for you," she says, and I appreciate it. I'm scared because I'm not sure what the right thing to do is. I wish she could tell me.

I do the only thing I know how to do. I run away.

I pick up my suitcase and walk out towards the front door. Everyone but Justin is in the kitchen, and they all say their goodbyes. I'm too exhausted to provide any answers or explanations.

"Rose, I'll email you those photos," I promise, giving them one last smile which doesn't quite reach my eyes, as I wave weakly. Rose rushes over to me and gives me a hug, squeezing me tightly.

"Maybe stay and have some food before you go?" She checks the time, anxiously biting her bottom lip.

"I can't." She nods as her shoulders sag in defeat.

"Take care of yourself. Please keep in touch," she says, hugging me again. I was never usually a tactile person, but I truly need this.

I wipe away my tears and turn away from them, my heart breaking. My heart aches because I can't say goodbye to Justin, but I understand why he isn't here. I was so horrible to him.

"Tell Justin I'm sorry," I whisper to Rose. She nods, sniffling. This is harder than I thought, but I'm going to walk out of the house, head held high.

I get into the taxi, not looking back. I can't.

I realise he is the same taxi driver who brought me here. I recognise him when I see his Santa Claus bobble head.

I tell him where to take me and sit back in the seat, crying. My heart aches. I truly felt part of the family, and now I'm ripping myself away.

"You okay, miss?" the taxi driver asks. I nod, but I'm not okay. He doesn't question me again, and we ride in silence. Once I can finally breathe again, I call my dad to let him know I will be home later today.

"Hey, Dad." I say and immediately start crying.

"Holly? What's wrong? What happened?" he asks, frantic.

"No, nothing happened. I'm just a mess, Dad."

"Honey, of course you're not a mess. We all make mistakes. I know I do!" he says, and that makes me cry more. I can see the strange looks that I am getting from the taxi driver, but I don't care.

"What's wrong?" Dad asks, and I don't want to hide it anymore.

I tell him everything. From how I felt when I lost my mum, and how I felt when Sara came into the picture. I tell him about how I came to hate my name, and wish Christmas wasn't a holiday, because it reminded me of my mother. I tell him how I resent myself for the way I've acted to everyone, so I avoid everything and everyone, and it all spills out into a colossal mess.

But, of course, he understands.

"Oh, darling, you know you've always been welcome here. Sara is not trying to replace your mum, and she never will. I was left alone as well when she died, and Sara helped immensely. I'm sorry I didn't know how you felt," he says, his voice strained.

"No, it's not your fault. It never was. I cut myself off from everything when she died, and now I know I was wrong," I say, wiping my nose on my sleeve.

"Darling, go back. I'll be here whenever you need me, and I think you'll find everything you need there." He says the exact same thing as Marilyn, and I know what I have to do. My mind clears, and my chest feels lighter. In typical Dad fashion, he told me exactly what I needed to hear. We hang up, and I can finally breathe again.

"Turn around, please!" I beg the driver. He turns around, muttering about how it was going to cost me.

"That's fine, just take me back. Please," I beg.

CHAPTER THIRTEEN

"Miss?" The driver slows down as I sit staring out of the window, biting my nails, wondering what I am going to say to Justin when I see him again.

Why wasn't he driving faster?

"Yeah?" Not completely listening.

"There's a man standing in front of the car."

My heart skips a beat and my muscles tense as I fling myself towards the middle of the car, trying to see who it is through the windscreen.

Justin.

He's standing outside, waiting for me. He's wearing his large coat, and flashing Christmas jumper, and I could not be more happy to see him.

I fling myself out of the taxi, and almost slip on black ice, but catch myself on the taxi door.

"See? One lesson from me, and you're a natural," Justin jokes, walking closer to me. I don't know what to say to him, so I stay quiet, staring at every feature of him. It scares me to think I was never going to see him again, but here he is.

Justins face falls slightly. "You came back," he says. I nod, still not knowing what to say, and not entirely trusting my voice to be steady.

"Why?" he asks, his voice breaking slightly. Just hearing his voice makes me tear up and want to rush to give him a hug. But I stay still.

"Aren't you going to say something, Grace?-Holly, damn. I will have to get used to that," he mutters. I walk towards him slowly, ignoring the driver's questions about when I would get back in the taxi, or if he should drive away. I can't speak.

"I-" I try to tell Justin everything he needs to know, but he reaches towards me, gently caresses my neck, and pulls me in.

He kisses me with such passion, I don't hear the driver take my luggage out of the boot and pull away. Sweet kisses begin to slow as Justin threads his hands through my hair, holding me closer to him. He lifts me from the floor, and I slip my arms around his neck, clinging to his muscular form trying to ground myself through the dizzying kiss. I never want to come up for air again.

His lips leave mine, but I'm not without them for long as he gently presses them to my cheek. I shiver and shut my eyes tightly as his lips make a trail along my temple, to my eyelids, to the tip of my nose, and back to my lips again. I'm melting like snow under his touch.

He gently pulls away, still holding me. He presses his forehead against mine and our breaths inter-twine.

"Did I make you fall in love with Christmas?" he asks, giving me another peck on the lips. I am com-pletely and utterly addicted.

"Yeah, you did," I answer, wanting to say that he made me fall for him too, but I know it's too soon for such certainties. I want to enjoy him and figure out whatever this is. I'm tired of living my life taking no risks and always choosing the safe option, so I've de-cided that Justin will be my first leap of faith in a new outlook on life

"What do you win? I just realised that we never said what my forfeit would be if I lost." I ask.

"Your happiness and the knowledge that I helped you," In that moment, I want nothing more than to kiss him again. I pause for a moment before realising that I can do just that. Leaning towards him, I lick my lips and close my eyes, waiting for his lips to meet mine.

My phone vibrates, and I, regrettably, wiggle myself out of his arms, attempting to ignore his waiting lips. Every fibre of my being wants to keep on kissing him and ignore my phone, but after so many years of relying on it, I find it difficult to ignore.

"It might be my dad," I say, laughing as Justin tries to pull me in for another kiss.

I look at my phone and laugh. It's the taxi driver.

I show Justin.

'I will charge you for my time. I have your number. Good luck with your fella.'

***

One Year Later... 25th December

The snow is graciously falling outside of Justin's bedroom window as my alarm rings, telling me it is *finally* Christmas day. I'm vibrating with excitement as I can't wait for the festivities, and everything that comes with it.

My heart flutters and my lips automatically smile as Justin stirs next to me, wrapping his strong arms around me and pulling me in close.

"Merry Christmas, gorgeous." His voice is warm and smooth, like his homemade hot chocolate.

"Merry Christmas." I turn around and kiss him, wondering how I got so lucky. I've had one whole year with him, and I've experienced the happiest moments of my life in that time.

I can hear people pottering around downstairs as they prepare for today's festivities.

"I'm so happy I found you," Justin whispers in my ear, gently stroking my hair. I almost melt like a snowflake as my heart clenches at his words. I didn't know I would find someone who wants to fix all of my broken pieces. He understands me and that is all I've ever wanted.

"I'm so happy we found each other," I say, nuzzling into his neck. He hugs me tighter and kisses my forehead as we lie in bed, relishing in the small piece of alone time.

The calm, quiet moment doesn't last long.

"Come on, you lovebirds! We have things to do!" Rose calls from outside the door. I laugh, knowing we won't be able to hide in here for much longer.

"Coming!" Justin shouts, giving me another kiss on the head.

"Mmhm," Rose mutters before I hear her footsteps skipping across the landing.

"Come on, we better go downstairs and help with the food preparations," I say, pulling the quilt off of me and shivering once the heat from the bed and Justin are no longer clinging to me.

"I want to give you my present first," he says, his eyes gleaming with joy. I nod, glad he wants to give it to me in private. It isn't because I'm embarrassed to open his present in front of family, it's because I love the thought of keeping certain things private. Just for us.

I hold my hand out and close my eyes, smirking.

"It's outside, actually," he says, chuckling at my excitement.

I frown. What could be outside? Although I am sceptical, I don't want to waste any time before getting my present. Jumping off the bed, I dash around the room, throwing on my clothes, occasionally stopping to kiss Justin. I throw on the Christmas jumper that Sara bought me last year, the jeans Rose and I bought on one of our many shopping trips, the snow boots I always wanted that were a gift from Justin, and finally, a warm, cosy scarf that Marilyn had knitted me.

"I'm ready. Take me to my gift," I say dramatically. Justin laughs, putting on the hat my Dad bought him on their first fishing trip together. He takes my hand and escorts me through our bedroom door after he picks up a backpack from the chair.

We manage to slip out through the back door quietly. The snow has eased up, but it is still falling, drifting gently down to the ground. I have grown to love the snow, and even wish it snowed more in the UK.

"Do you remember the day we first met?" Justin asks. He doesn't look at me, and I want him to, if only to get a hint about where he is going with this. I love his eyes, and the way his dimples will show every time he smiles or laughs, but I especially love how he can never keep his emotions from showing on his face.

"I do. I remember missing the train and having to practically beg for a taxi!" I laugh at the memory, "And I remember your incredibly cheesy Christmas jumper and when your car boot jammed!" I'm shocked that it all happened over a year ago. It seems like just yesterday.

"I knew you were different when you determinedly fixed my car tyre by yourself in a blizzard, even though you hate the cold. And when you told me that you hated, sorry...*disliked* Christmas music, I knew that knowing you would be a rollercoaster ride." He finally stops beside the lake. It's frozen over, and I have the urge to skate across. I always do when we come here.

"I remember when you told me that you had never skated before, and I remember the joy on your face when you stood out on that lake by yourself. You looked breathtakingly beautiful," he says, his eyes glistening slightly.

"Are you okay?" I ask, gently touching his cheek. He nods, biting his lower lip nervously and I can see that he is clenching and unclenching his hands.

"I'm more than okay, Holly. I just..." He pauses, taking his gloves off and looking towards the lake.

"Do you fancy skating?" he asks and I nod, watching him pull two pairs of skates from his bag, his hands shaking. I'm not sure if that is from the cold or from whatever is clearly making him nervous. As I watch him, he seems somehow distant and I rack my brains as to what could be bothering him.

In the meantime, I pull my skates on as Justin holds me up, and we glide on the lake. Justin's hands never leave mine as we skate in a comfortable silence, the snow starting to fall heavier than before.

Justin stops, and pulls me closer to him.

"Holly," he whispers, looking straight into my eyes.

"Justin, what's going on?" I squeeze his hands tighter, hoping they provide some comfort.

"I love you more than anything in this world. When I first met you, I thought you were beautiful and incredible and independent, despite the hands you've been dealt. You inspired me from day one." His voice shakes with nerves.

"And I love you. You made me a better person and helped me to move on. You are my Christmas miracle," I reply, touching his cheek. He looks down, relief and love permeating his expression, and takes a deep breath.

"Holly, I will love you and protect you for the rest of my life. You have my word." he promises, his eyes boring into mine. I say nothing, beginning to realise where this is going.

Without hesitating, Justin pulls a red box from his jacket pocket and attempts to get down on one knee, slipping slightly on the ice. I gasp, my hands covering my mouth as I realise I'm going to be asked one of the most important questions of my life.

"It's very hard to kneel on ice…" he mutters, as he finally manages to do it. I laugh, desperate to hear those words from his lips. Justin looks at me, smiling with tears in his eyes.

"Will you marry me, Holly Grace Taylor?" He opens the tiny, red box. Inside is the most exquisite ring I have ever seen.

My entire world seems to explode around me. I sob, kneeling down beside him, taking his face in my hands, and looking deep into his eyes.

"Yes! I would say yes to you in a million life-times!" I cry. He shuts his eyes and covers his mouth with his spare hand, letting my answer sink in.

"I was hoping you'd say that," he says, his voice trembling. He reaches into the box, pulling out the gorgeous ring and gently placing it onto my left ring finger.

I look up to the sky and hope that my mother is watching. I hope she is seeing how I've found my safe place, and that she doesn't have to worry about me anymore.

I look back at Justin, and I know. This is the beginning of the rest of our lives.

And I can't wait.

THE END

ABOUT THE AUTHOR

Stephanie Jane O'Neil is a 23-year-old author from South Wales. *Picture Not So Perfect* is her debut release.

Stephanie's love for books and writing began while studying at Caerleon Comprehensive school. She would later fall in love with creative writing whilst at college before achieving a scholarship to study at Aberystwyth University. This is where she truly developed her writing skills and acquired a deeper appreciation for the written word. Stephanie left Aberystwyth after three years of study with a BA Honours Second Class Degree in English Literature.

Picture Not So Perfect is the first of many stories by Stephane Jane O'Neil to hold a space on your book shelf, with many more in planning. To keep up to date with all future news and releases, follow Stephanie online at:

Instagram / Twitter: *@steph_author*

Website: *www.stephaniejaneoneil.com*

Printed in Great Britain
by Amazon

70482154R00088